SAME SEX

Gay SF Clone Erotica

J. W. STEED
FRANK SLATER

Introduction by
PETER SCHUTES

CONTENTS

INTRODUCTION

BY PETER SCHUTES

I am the present-day author/publisher behind the character and nom de plume, Peter Schutes. As a child and teen in the 1970s and early 1980s, I used to pore over and devour my father's bookshelves which were lined with Science Fiction pulp paperbacks by the likes of Isaac Asimov, Robert A. Heinlein, Aldous Huxley, C. S. Lewis, Philip K. Dick, Ray Bradbury, and a host of smaller names that were experts at the genre. I was fascinated by the imagination of the authors and captivated by the ideas of space travel, telepathy, book burning, colonization, aliens, and, yes, cloning.

As a young budding homosexual, I had a strange fetish that arose out of fear of my desires. I believed that if I could clone one of my secret crushes, I would have a clandestine lover without exposure to the cruelty of classmates. I wouldn't have to worry about the horrifying aftermath of rejection, for this clone wouldn't attend my school. He'd just be mine. It was a little creepy now that I committed the notion to paper.

What I wouldn't have given to read a queer Science Fiction book back then. In those times, queer rights were newly born. Our sexuality was still codified as a crime in many states, and we had only just been removed from the *Diagnostic and Statistical Manual of Mental Disorders (DSM)*. This didn't stop so many brave pulp authors from creating erotica, but it was hidden under counters, forbidden to a young reader. And my father was not interested in anything remotely queer, so his Sci-Fi shelf was heteronormative, to use a more modern adjective that wasn't available back then.

I shoplifted my first gay romance, "An Idol for Others" by Gordon Merrick. Shaking with fear, I tucked the book into my knapsack and ran out of Waldenbooks like a jackrabbit. By the time I finished reading the book, it was in poor condition, with several pages adhered to one another. And it wasn't the least bit speculative, other than the preposterous size of the male members that cousins Peter and Charlie had inherited.

How surprised was I when J. W. Steed and Frank Slater, two outstanding authors, both proposed queer, erotic Science Fiction stories about clones? I was bowled over! Both of these stories arrived on my review desk at the same time. I had only asked if they had any SF up their sleeves. If you believe in something beyond coincidence, then perhaps the hairs on your arm will also stand up in salute as mine did.

Journey's End resides in the space colonization subgenre, with a very queer take on narcissism. The many variations of the protagonist have served their corporation well. It is only fair that they service one another.

Billy Club takes place in a small, gritty city. Law enforcement in this town is brutal, sadistic, and very queer. The force is divided between regular cops and a team of same-sex lookalikes. Our heroes know just what it takes to please a cop, and it isn't just a donut.

Like its predecessor, *Cosmic Cage*, this duology was

conceived originally as a tête-bêche, a book that, when flipped lengthwise, has a different cover and story. Many science fiction pulps in the days of dime novels were constructed this way. If I went to a custom printer, I might be able to create such a magical book. But in the world of modern print-on-demand book sales, with UPC labels and automatic proofreading censors, the technology of the future has made it nearly impossible.

A brief word on censorship and book-burning. As of the writing of this introduction, in one week, we will peacefully hand over the reins to a new authoritarian regime in the United States. According to their work of (hopefully) Speculative Fiction, *Project 2025*, they seek to revive the Comstock Act, a book-burning law that has remained unenforced for over a century. It prohibits the distribution of erotic materials that are deemed lewd or lascivious. This law also prohibits the distribution of materials associated with contraception, which is the primary reason for re-awakening the zombie law. This law led to actual book burning in the past, and it will lead to a federal ban on the distribution of contraception pills and erotica of all kinds in the present.

We may be about to enter the Gilead era of our formerly free country. If you haven't read *The Handmaid's Tale*, I suggest you do so immediately upon finishing this text. This may be the last book Peter Schutes Publishing produces. Your publisher could find himself hanging from 'the wall' along with other gender traitors.

I hope that *Same Sex* not only sees the light of day but that it also serves as a beacon of First Amendment freedoms, forever shining in the canon of queer literature! Let us ensure that *Fahrenheit 451* and *1984* remain works of fiction. Democracy is fragile.

JOURNEY'S END

BY J. W. STEED

ACKNOWLEDGMENTS

I must thank Peter Schutes for the fun and fruitful opportunity to collaborate with him on these anthologies. Erotica is an art form too often shunted to the margins, but Peter knows how to package it playfully. My friend Grey assisted with helpful suggestions on an early draft of the story, and my friend Al lent his valuable insights—as well as his endless supply of dad jokes. I extend my gratitude to all you fine gentlemen! - J.W. Steed

One face, one voice, one habit, and two persons,
A natural perspective that is and is not!
– William Shakespeare
Twelfth Night, Act 5, Scene 1

Jerzemy's left on his Show-Me again.

I understand. Shutting down my console with voice commands is an old habit of mine, too. Out here on the frontier, or even high above the planet on Illyria Orbital where Jerzemy is posted, however, we don't have the automations and luxuries of back home. I'm not complaining about the accommodations, mind you. Life on a terraforming outpost means always balancing the expense of bleeding-edge technology with ever-stringent United Settlements budgets. Something has to give. That's why our Show-Mes have always been cobbled together from discarded circuit boards, lengths of vacuum-grade duct tape, and a prayer.

Honestly, though, Jerzemy. Mechanical switches might be primitive technology, but they're not that difficult! Up and down. Down and up. Two directions! One switch for the incoming displays. Another for the imagers that let us view each other. A third for data flow, which we both usually leave on during the planet's thirteen-hour night. A fourth for the embedded mics. At the end of our catch-up moments before, I'd heard him issue a shutdown command and flip off the speakers and visuals as he pushed back his chair. Then he'd walked away, not realizing he was still live.

I tap on the center screen and call his name, trying to get his attention before he reaches his living quarters beyond. He can't hear or see me, though I've got full volume on his sleepy yawn, his shuffling feet on the hab floor, then the off-screen whine of the bathroom sonics. He's taking a shower before bed.

Well, we've both had a long day.

Mine tend to be longer than Jerzemy's. The success of this project depends on me. And it will be a success. We have another week of seeding these saline lakes with microbes before the skimmer is scheduled to head inland. Preparing the local environment to accept and sustain basins of potable water is a process that can't be rushed. Good old H_2O. The building block of life itself. Bringing life is our mission on Illyria, fourth planet from the star Denebola.

I chuckle a little to hear Jerzemy break out into song. A few seconds pass before I place it: an ancient love ballad from before the great diaspora. In Jerzemy's strong baritone, it rings all the louder among the bathroom tiles. Our father used to sing this particular tune to our mother when he was in a romantic mood. The coy smiles they'd share when they thought I wasn't looking! He'd croon the verse to her over a handful of posies from the greenhouse. She'd swat at him, and then together, they'd giggle their way to the bedroom, where I wasn't supposed to know what went on.

I wandered around, and I finally found the somebody who...

Years it's been since I thought of Dad courting Mom with that sweet, old-fashioned melody. What could have triggered Jerzemy's memory? Surely, he can't be in love. I should turn off the feeds, let him sing in peace. Really, I'm spying. But Jerzemy occupies my old quarters aboard the orbital, and I remain a touch territorial over my former digs. Though I still maintain attention on readings from the skimmer poised above the lake basin, I can't help but notice Jerzemy padding back into the living area completely naked save for a white towel around his waist.

He's still singing. *Could make me be true—could make me feel blue.*

I chuckle, because there's no water with a sonic scrub—yet out of habit, I also wear a towel after showering. What creatures of habit we both are.

My former hab is in one of the orbital's older, original sections, attached to the corridors by an airlock with paired hand-cranked bulkheads. I hear someone wrangling with the outer wheel. I recall that sound well. Who's visiting, though? I'd watch to see, but the Show-Me flashes a query from Logistics.

"Director's office. Go ahead." I know who it is without having to look up.

There's a pause, then a baritone rumble. "You still up, Jeremy?" That would be Jerry, my right-hand man down here.

"Of course, he's still up. Have you ever seen the man sleep?" The deeper voice belongs to Bald Jerry, lounging next to him behind the desk. I suppose you'd call Bald Jerry my left-hand man. The two are rarely seen apart. Both are A-class, so they wear the mandatory United Settlements coveralls. Branded, of course, with our sponsor's logo: a stylized cowboy hat with the Rancho Buck's name superimposed. Though they look alike, Jerry's the one with long dark hair pulled into a ponytail; Bald Jerry—well, we gave him the nickname for a reason, though to be literal, he shaves his head. "Jeremy doesn't even eat. He absorbs nutrients from the ether, like an air fern."

Jerry corrects him. "*Air fern* is a misnomer. The historical phenomenon was neither a fern nor did it..."

"Jerzemy and I were conferencing," I say to cut short the lecture. "What's up?"

"A hundred and eighty-five asteroid miners walk into

a bar." Oh no. Situation dismal. The Jerrys have got jokes. "And the bartender says, sorry, we don't serve miners here. And the miners say..."

Bald Jerry began cultivating a handlebar mustache once we all were planetside. After five months, it looks utterly ridiculous. He waggles the abomination comically while leaning in to deliver the punchline. "...Minors? We're all *over twenty-one and have the U.S. subcutaneous implants to prove it!*"

"Hilarious." I don't even look up from the skimmer readings.

"He didn't like it," says Bald Jerry. "Okay. The next one's better. Tell him."

I hear Jerry clear his throat. "A hundred and eighty-five orbital viewport glaziers walk into a bar..."

Yeah, I'm certain this one will be *much* better.

But I'm not even listening, because on the center display, Jerzemy's visitor steps into view. I recognize Benny, work rucksack slung over a shoulder. Benny, my boyfriend—no. Benny, my ex. My former boyfriend, who should have no reason to visit this section of the orbital.

Still, I can't help but smile.

He's so beautiful, my boy. Even in that atrocious red-and-white Rangers jumpsuit with the distinctive cowboy hat logo across its back. He's kept lean and fit in the orbital's gymnasium. His beard has grown fuller —blonder, too?—over the last few months. I have missed those baby blue eyes, that messy blond mop atop his head. Those pouty lips. Those perfect, round buttocks. I may be a man of science, but I have needs. Seeing Benny after five months accelerates them into overdrive.

Why is he in my old quarters, though?

I watch, heart pounding, as Jerzemy and Benny move close. For a split second, they stare into each other's eyes with meaning. "No," I whisper in disbelief, on my side of the display. Benny's curls tumble as he removes his branded white Stetson. Jerzemy, the big brute, stoops down to allow the boy to set it upon his head.

Benny grins, then gives the brim a flick. "I missed you today, cowboy," I hear him say.

My guts heave in turmoil. Today had been routine and placid—until this. I hold my breath, willing what is about to happen, not to.

"...Oh well, we're gonna leave anyway, 'cause this joint ain't all it's *cracked up* to be!" Both Jerrys erupt in raucous laughter that I cut off with a flick of a switch.

"Sorry, gentlemen," I stammer to the Jerrys, unable to tear my eyes away. That bastard Jerzemy, with a cocky angle to his concrete jaw, is hooking his finger beneath the towel's makeshift knot. It falls to the floor. He stands completely unclothed before Benny and holds out his arms. Welcoming him. Wanting him. "Director's office, signing off for the night." Their square faces disappear with the flick of another switch.

With both helplessness and rage, I watch Benny allow another man to take him into his embrace. Jerzemy pulls him hard and close to his naked body, pressing him into that sonicked, sweet-smelling chest fur. They sway back and forth, slow dancing to Jerzemy's crooning.

It had to be you. Wonderful you. It had to be...you.

Benny tilts his head back. He gazes up at the older man, breathless. Even from this distance, I can see stars in his eyes. "I need you inside me," he whispers, almost as if he were in my own arms.

Jerzemy strokes the boy's cheek, then nuzzles him closer. "Oh, I think I can oblige."

That's when I beat against the console and yell, "No! *Benny, no!*" But I'm punishing myself more than I am the Show-Me. They're built to last. Back and forth I rock in my chair, nursing the bruised and sore heel of my hand, as helplessly I witness Jerzemy unzip Benny's jumpsuit and peel it down, slowly and with intent, until the boy stands naked and erect before him.

Damn it to all hell, I think, unable to tear my eyes away.

How long has my ex-boyfriend been fucking my clone?

Jerzemy sits upon the bed, his back protected from the chilly hab wall by a propped-up pillow. His—my—*our* thick, meaty thighs are spread wide, knees bent, heels digging into the mattress. So strange, seeing myself naked like that. Clones in the lesser classes—like the two A-class Jerrys and the multiple C-class Jers manning the loading bays and the skimmer—tend to differentiate themselves from their original by altering their hairstyles or growing mustaches and beards. Sometimes, they'll accumulate piercings or accessories like spectacles or Tell-Me implants over their ears.

Jerzemy, though, is a rare S-class reproduction, an exact duplicate of myself made at unthinkable expense shortly before my deployment to Illyria five months ago. He shares not merely my appearance but all my memories, experiences, and expertise. My responsibilities as well.

An S-class clone hews close to its progenitor; it is created to share an especially heavy burden of authority. A jolt of electricity pricks my spine every time I zoom the imager upon that bed and recognize myself naked on that mattress: big jaw, broad stubbled face, brown eyes, coarse salt-and-pepper hair in waves. Old-world

Slav looks, with an old-world laborer's furry trunk and thick legs to match. I—*we*—look like a brute. A hairy devil, heavy-browed and glowering.

Like anyone, I'm accustomed to seeing myself reversed in a mirror. Every glance at Jerzemy, though, marries the familiar to the uncanny. Through the Show-Me, I view his body the same way the world looks at mine. The subtle difference always disturbs. That cock, though. Is that how it really appears, front-on? At this angle, it's monstrous. I've always known my fat kielbasa was more than a mouthful, though never has a sex partner complained about me being extra-large.

Looking at it now, though, zoomed in and expanded to occupy most of the projected display, the sight is staggering. Jerzemy has greased himself with lubricant. He grips his dick tightly around the base, first with one thick fist, then the other atop it. There's still more protruding over the top. When he releases it, the impressive beast jerks and throbs, pointing all the time at the hab ceiling. It's scarlet. Throbbing. Like Jerzemy's face, it's angry.

I want to look away, but I cannot. This is the third night cycle I've been glued to my console, spying upon my clone with the man I used to call my boyfriend. Three nights in a row, Jerzemy hasn't realized he's left the imager running. Three nights in a row, I've been forced to watch as he strips down to nothing and demands Benny's attentions.

Yet, have I really been forced? Deep inside, I know no one coerces me. What I'm doing is wrong. Flat-out, unmistakably wrong. I could easily flip off my own displays and head down to the mess for roast beef sandwiches with the Jerrys. I could get some work done. I could go to bed early, soothe these aching eyes. So many coulds and shoulds.

Let's shut this peep show down for the night, I decide.

Only then I catch my breath: Benny has emerged from the bathroom, freshly sonicked and scented. He pauses at the sight of Jerzemy stroking himself upon the bed. My finger trembles upon the switch for a moment.

Abandoning all good intentions, I lean in to watch.

"You want it?" Jerzemy growls. When Benny hesitates, he nods down at his engorged tool. "This fat blaster is fully charged. I said: do you want it?"

Benny faces away from me. He shifts his weight from one leg to the other, causing my heart to skip a beat. I zoom in and create a new frame focused on his pert, naked buttocks. "I just got cleaned up." Jerzemy isn't impressed with the boy's excuse. He looks from Benny down to his demanding erection, then back again. "I've barely gotten home. Can I get a drink or something?"

That's right. I'm cheerleading for Team Benny. *Turn down that motherfucker. Turn him down hard.* But part of me can't help but notice how Benny uses that word. *Home.* When did Benny move into Jerzemy's hab aboard the orbital? Was my bed even cool before it happened?

"I'll give you something to drink, all right." Jerzemy's voice slices through my thoughts like a hot knife. "Suck it."

There's a split second of hesitation in which I silently beseech the boy to resist, to break away from whatever thrall this monstrous clone has over him. It doesn't last.

"Yes, sir," Benny breathes, before dropping to his knees. Across the orbital floor, he shuffles until he reaches the bed's bottom. Up he climbs, smooth body sliding against shiny sheets. The edge of the mattress catches his hard dick and forces it down. It points toward his toes, in the direction of Jerzemy's console, flattened at an unnatural angle against the rumpled bedding between his thighs. Part of me mourns, witnessing my boy slithering, serpentine, toward his altar of profane worship.

Why do I even think of him as my boy? Five months have passed since we parted aboard the orbital. Can I expect a reconciliation when he's high above and I'm down below? Younger people are scarce up there. Inevitable, he should turn to an older man. Much as I want to ascribe some nefarious influence to my clone, it would be natural for Benny to share an attraction to him. An S-class clone is an exact physical dupe that shares ninety-eight percent of my neural cortex patterns. We differ exclusively in...well. I haven't thought about that much.

Essentially, Jerzemy is me. And Benny...well, he liked me. Used to. Past tense.

My ex plainly cannot resist that replica of my cock. But Jerzemy stops his advance by planting a sole on one of Benny's shoulders. "Not yet," he growls. "Feet, first." My view is of the back of Benny's head, but I imagine his face—big eyes gazing steadily at Jerzemy from beneath a spill of golden curls, his pouty lips pursed and ready for kissing. In my hand, my cock swells as I watch Benny spread his knees and squat, so he can take one of the clone's meaty calves in his hands. When the boy rasps his beard over Jerzemy's sole, my own feet twitch in sympathy. "That's right."

"Thank you, sir." The boy plants soft kisses—one, two, three—each making its way from heel to tip. His mouth opens; his soft tongue snakes out to twine around the clone's middle toe. His lips follow, wrapping themselves around the digit while the toes surrounding wriggle against his face. I watch with excitation as Jerzemy leans back. His hands interlock behind his head as he watches the boy work.

Benny opens his mouth a little wider, admitting a second toe, then a third. His lips pull into a grimace to take the fourth, then stretch to their widest to encompass that last big toe. Between his thighs, a puddle of precum stains the sheets. I wish he were worshiping my feet in this way. Slow. Sensual. Giving me a preview of how he'll soon suck and slobber over the dick.

"That's real nice," says the clone. His cock, like mine, still rages for attention. Yet when Benny reaches up to grab at it, Jerzemy swats away his hand. "Finish the job," he barks.

Across the display, I swipe, point, and beckon until feeds from the clone's imager fill all my Show-Me's tall displays. I spit into my fingers and spread the fluid around my meat, getting it slick. My eyes fix on Benny. Multiple Bennys, magnified to show off the parts of his body I like. There's the close-up of his ass I queued up earlier, so tightly zoomed I can see each clench and pucker of the hole he sucks the clone's toes. Benny's erection, dowsing up and down as he shifts position. Benny's shoulders—a young man's shoulders, strong and supple, confident enough to carry the burden of decades to come. Bennys everywhere before me, occupying every inch of my peripheral vision as I stroke.

The boy abandons one foot for the other, this time applying the flat of his tongue to the clone's sole. "So wet. That's how I like it." Jerzemy's voice rumbles low but audible from across the hab. "That's a sweet mouth."

The compliment makes the boy lick harder, as if that big peasant foot is candy for a sweet tooth. His lids open. Benny meets the clone's eyes as he announces, "I deserve to suck that cock now."

"Oh, you do?" Jerzemy sounds amused. He removes his foot from the boy's grasp and plants it onto the bed. Both his forearms rest upon his knees—the picture of casual masculine confidence. "Who says I'm going to let you?"

"I do." Hard as I am, my heart aches to hear Benny's next words. "That cock belongs to me. It's *mine.*"

Jerzemy's eyes glitter. "Yours, huh? Well. Better treat it right, then."

"Yes, sir." Given permission, Benny seizes the prize for which he's hungered. The moment the clone's dick leaps in the boy's clutch, my own strains for release. Beneath my clenched knuckles, my balls tighten and shift. Benny tilts back his neck so that his curls tease the nape. "I love you, sir," he whispers.

Imagers capture the two in perfect profile, face to face, across multiple frames upon my displays. Jeremy cups the boy's head and pulls him in for a long, deep kiss. I cannot deny my covetousness when I watch the clone's lips—my lips—completely surround Benny's. "Yeah? Prove it."

Oh, Benny. I would never have replied to your confession with that brutal challenge. Hearing my ex whisper intimacies to my clone should harden my heart. Yet transgression multiplies my excitement. My hand travels up and down my slick shaft with increasing speed.

Three nights of betrayal, I've witnessed. Three nights, I've climaxed with savage ferocity, watching the pair in secret.

Both of Jerzemy's hands dig deep into Benny's thick curls, drawing them back from the sides of his face as he guides the boy's mouth toward his dick. Then I startle: while my ex-boyfriend struggles to accommodate as much of that thick shaft as he can, the clone looks my way.

Not merely my way: from across the orbital hab, Jerzemy stares directly at the imager lens at the exact moment my cock erupts. Instinctively, I tamp down on my cries, afraid of being heard. I panic, certain that I've been caught in my surveillance. Too late. Semen already sprays the back of my knuckles. On every display, while Benny chokes and gurgles on the clone's shaft, from nearly two thousand kilometers somewhere overhead, Jerzemy's eyes bore into my own.

Only when my orgasm and the roar of arousal and panic in my ears subside do I realize an alarm blares. A Code 37 alert from the skimmer out on the local saline lakes: an electrical fault in the braking system.

Jerzemy must be hearing the same alarm. He isn't looking at me, of course, but across the hab at his own console. While Benny sucks happily, Jerzemy waits to see if the warning whine is something to which he needs to attend. I'm about to do something myself when the noise subsides and the frame changes from red to green. One of the Jers aboard the skimmer must have fixed whatever went wrong.

Above and around me on every surface of smooth glass, Benny issues small noises of self-satisfaction as he services the clone's empurpled and glistening shaft. I'm still too shaken to continue watching. One by one, I flip the toggles to cancel the feed.

Then I push back my chair and search for a towel to wipe away proof of my misdeed. What I'm doing is wrong. Every instinct warns me to stop.

I worry, however, that I cannot.

❧ 3 ❧

Benny Dahl was all of twenty-three when I met him, four years ago. I had just turned thirty-nine. It was months before the second wave of the great pandemic, during a two-week layover on Deimos, when I still headed a crew of forty scientists. All of us assembled to wait for the arrival of the United Settlements jump ship that would transport our group and equipment out to this sector of the galaxy. Our group was so eager to start transforming Illyria into a habitat suitable for humankind.

Deimos has always been a shithole underground way station burrowed in a shithole moon, visited only by people on their way to better places, occupied by impoverished folk destined never to see anything civilized. Benny was the son of miners, determined to become an influencer through sheer force of will. He hawked for some sort of novelty boba liquor brand but really was little more than a barback. I'd caught his eye in the port lounge my very first night cycle. We stayed up late in the bar, talking. And then, naked later in my quarters, not talking at all.

For the first time, I—Dr. Jeremy Wollny, with terminal degrees in both exobotany and geophysics—was a man on fire. The boy kept me in constant heat. I

20

couldn't get my fill of him. I even made discreet inquiries about staying on Deimos, of all the godforsaken places. The Eli de la Torre Foundation, the Illyria project's co-sponsor at the time, would hear none of it. When my team and I shipped off, I promised to get Benny out of that backwater as soon as I could arrange.

Part of me wondered if I was being used by a pretty boy with a pretty smile who was desperate to get his especially pretty ass off a barren rock known solely for its jump station and prisons.

The other part of me was grateful to be used.

Months later, I managed to find my obsession a berth on a small jump ship transporting medical supplies. Rumors of viral resurgence were beginning to spread right when he left port; by the time he arrived in Spica, the second wave was in full force. Benny passed the next two years in lockdown—three months of it in barren Spica aboard that jump ship, the rest in a quarantine facility orbiting Arcturus Prime. He'd spent the entire duration isolated with that ship's captain. I know their relationship was sexual. Two years is a long time. How could I object?

It's not, then, as if we've always been sexually exclusive. Toward the end of that lockdown, when restrictions were lifting and after I'd lost three-quarters of my team, I myself had taken up with a friendly young man who'd delivered supplies to my airlock during sequester. Benny and I never had a formal arrangement. We never discussed or registered a union. He'd always said I was married to my work. He has clearly moved on.

But why did he have to move on with my exact genetic duplicate?

I'm mulling it over, chewing on a fistful of pemmican, when the Jerrys join me in the mess. "What up, Dr. J!" Jerry attempts to involve me in some kind of complicated handshake. I give up after two baffling iterations.

Bald Jerry merely bestows a nod and observes what

I'm eating. "I'm making a frittata, if you want to join us."

Bald Jerry can do some amazing things with boxed eggs, potato cakes, a few veggies, and Bucky Sauce. "Yes, please!" I say, grateful to have an excuse to abandon the dried protein.

"Jeremy." Jerry is tugging at my sleeve. "Jeremy! Knock-knock." I don't immediately reply, so he prompts in a stage whisper, "You're supposed to say, *who's there.*"

Oh, gods. It's too early for Jerry jokes. "Who's there?"

"Laika."

"Laika who?"

"I Laika you a lot. So open up the airlock and let me in." Behind me, in the kitchen area, Bald Jerry lets out a snort. I even hear a few whuffs of amusement from the several Jers at a table nearby. When I fail to bray the laughter he seems to feel his jape deserves, he leans in. "You see, Laika was the first dog in space. Back on Earth."

"1957 in Old Calendar years, I believe," says Bald Jerry, making things sizzle.

"Yes," I say, distracted by the delicious smells already wafting from his way. "The best jokes are always the ones you afterward need to explain in exhaustive detail. Hey," I add, struck by a thought. "Do you two remember Benny?"

A genuine smile softens Jerry's lips. "Benny."

From the cooktop, Bald Jerry sighs. "Benny."

Is it my imagination, or does the sound of Benny's name bring a sudden stillness to the chatter of the Jers nearby?

"We liked Benny." Jerry looks at Bald Jerry for confirmation. "Didn't we?"

"We did. Sweet boy, Benny. Though I can't recall..."

I take their vagueness as a given. Not much of my

past emotional life would have transferred to an A-class clone, though some imprint would remain. Jerry and Bald Jerry are quality replications—far more faithful to my mental pattern than the Jers they've generated since —but little attention goes into imprinting their nonessential neural connections. Cheaper that way. The Jerrys probably have vague positive feelings toward my Benny, but no real memories. And the Jers, the copies of the copies? To them, a mention of Benny's name would be no more than a flash of spring sunshine on a cloudy day.

"If I'm not being too forward, may I ask..." Already, I regret my train of thought.

I've got their attention, though. "Jeremy. We're here to help." Maybe the shaved dome gives him an air of wisdom, because I believe Bald Jerry.

"Anything," promises Jerry, dropping the class clown act. They wait in expectation.

I force out the words. "What is it you do for...you know. Relief?"

"One of the Jers has a sideline as a massage therapist," Jerry says, looking around for the clone in question. "We could book you a session."

Bald Jerry clears his throat. "I think the chief means *sexual* relief."

"Ohhhh," Jerry replies. The pair exchange a look so intimate that I regret asking. There's no law against clones pleasuring each other. I'm sure it happens more often than I care to imagine. Yet, to me, it feels offensive. Incestuous. "No." Jerry at once judges by my stink-face what I'm thinking. "We don't fuck. It's all porn on the Show-Me."

"Lots of porn."

"All the porn," Jerry confirms. "But..." He exchanges a look with Bald Jerry that clearly reads as *May I tell him?* "We'll watch the same titles at the same time. In our own habs."

"Then we compare notes. See which parts I liked that he didn't. We find it interesting to see how we differ."

I'm confused. "You don't...we don't like the same things?"

"Chief, an A-class is imprinted with only what, forty-five percent of the original's brain patterns?" Jerry looks to Bald Jerry for confirmation. "That doesn't make us only forty-five percent of a real person. The rest fills itself in. Bald Jerry's planning on taking up fishing once we populate the lakes. I, on the other hand, am honing my burgeoning talent for stand-up."

"Nature abhors a vacuum." Bald Jerry pours liquid egg from a carton. "And Jerry's jokes. You seem surprised?"

"Perhaps I am? I don't know. Genetically, we're identical. Not similar. The same."

"Ah," says Bald Jerry, tapping his nose. "Yet hundreds of patterns can be cut from a single bolt of cloth."

"Look at the C-class clones." Jerry's lecture mode is the same as my own: brisk and commonsensical. "Twenty-five percent of the original's brain structure. The technical bits. Yet the Jers show more diversity among themselves than Bald Jerry and I do. Far more than you and Jerzemy. Jer, over there, plays the balalaika at a nearly-professional level. That Jer by the window is working on a screenplay in his spare time. The Jer across from him..."

"Back to the point: no. We don't like the same porn. Often, we do." Bald Jerry shoves his pan in the Cook-Me for a quick convection blast, waggling his brows at Jerry in some sort of private joke. "I've been very much into restraints lately."

"Rough sex."

"The rougher, the better." The unit finishes the blast cycle and beeps. Our chef mitts up and removes the frittata, filling the room with a scent that overpowers the ever-lingering aroma of vat-grown roast beef and curly fries. "And Jerry love love *loves* bi scenes."

"MMF is so damned hot." Jerry's retrieved a few forks and knives for the table during our conversation. "I know it's not your thing," he apologizes. "Are these questions about Benny?"

The most I'll reveal is what a sad shrug conveys. Bald Jeremy brings his steaming frittata to the table and cuts me a wedge. "Eat up, chief," he suggests, pulling up a chair. "You need real food. A fellow can't live on ration bars."

"Such a handsome kid. Wasn't it Benny who got us the Rancho Buck's sponsorship?"

I nod through a savory gulp. Post-pandemic, Eli de la Torre and his foundation had pulled out of the Illyria project. The population drop in the colonized sectors meant that supporting existing settlements was a greater foundational priority than establishing new ones.

It truly was touch and go until Benny stepped in, the very week we reunited on the orbital. His competition largely wiped out, he parlayed his negligible influencer background into a real talent for brand representation. With some clever negotiation for perpetual planetary fast food rights, endorsement, and exclusive progress reports via the chain's Show-Me feeds, within days, we gained a new sponsor. We officially rebranded as Illyria's Planetary Preparation Rangers Co-sponsored by United Settlements Conservation Corps and Rancho Buck's Mighty Roast Beef Sandwiches. (Yes, it's a mouthful.)

Substrate branding, they call what's now upon the syllabus of every institution of advanced business education, from New Cornell to École Arcturus. Imprinting the client's brand from the bedrock up. Benny himself coined the term.

"Thank gods he did." I'd imported someone I'd

thought of as ornamental, thinking I was rescuing him —only to have his business acumen save the project I'd been laboring upon for a decade. The irony is not lost upon me. The boy's branding deals will, in the end, make him a great deal wealthier than ever I will be. He won't need my aid to see all the worlds of which he dreamed, back on Deimos.

I savor the taste of real food while I mull it over. Jerry drags me from my complacency by tapping a finger on my forehead. "Okay. One hundred and eighty-five space walkers walk into a bar. And the bartender says…"

Bald Jerry does the next bit. "We don't serve space walkers here."

Jerry continues. "And the space walkers say…"

I lean back in my chair, cross my arms, and supply the obvious punchline. "That's okay; we were gonna leave because we *didn't like the atmosphere*." I break out into booming laughter while the Jerrys pull faces at each other.

"Did we tell him that one already?" asks Jerry.

Bald Jerry shrugs. "No. But it's a really dumb joke."

Still chuckling, I study my two lookalikes with a sudden burst of affection. Maybe we're not as different as they think.

"**Y**ou look drawn, Jeremy." Far above on the orbital, Jerzemy leans in to cock his head and peer at me. I observe his nose hairs and make a mental note to trim my own.

For a moment, my rival's words barely register. "Fine. Still not accustomed to the Illyrian day cycle." Rarely have I fibbed so smoothly or with such an insincere smile. I might even be overacting the part. "Anything else we need to cover?" Two hours this morning we've spent comparing notes as the skimmer prepares to move inland. We are officially prepped with the barrage of microbes engineered to transform this particular soil type into arable land.

Journey's End, I've informally named the biome—the most promising spot for a first settlement on this continent.

Jerzemy's involvement with Benny, for lack of a better word, hasn't affected our working relationship. My clone and I are not required to be buddies. Ever since his replication, we've discussed nothing but business. This comment about my appearance may very well be the first personal question he's ever asked.

"Nothing at my end," he says, fiddling with something on his display. "I've got that committee meeting later with the Corps HQ. Arcturan afternoon for them, nighttime for us. I'll report back after."

Delegating dull committee meetings is probably the best reason to have a double. I'm perfectly happy to head up science personnel on the ground while he deals with bureaucratic red tape up there. My eyes maintain a watch on the screen long enough to verify he's not going to flip off the damned Show-Me switches. Should I say something? Call attention to his oversight? At this point I'm embarrassed I should have to. I also worry if I do, he'll deduce I've seen something I shouldn't.

I wheel my chair around. "Over and out." I pointedly make a show of toggling off my own feed, saving my imager for last. Maybe he'll get the hint. There. Not so hard, Jerzemy. Resolved not to stick my nose in the affairs of my ex, no matter how tempting, I start the day's work.

For a good few hours, I succeed in keeping away from the displays. We clean out the skimmer's tanks and refill them with new microbe-bearing reagents. The skimmer's braking system develops another of its damned faults, but the Jers and I manage to fix it on our own. After Bald Jerry cobbles together roast beef pizzas for everyone using raw ingredients from our sponsor's food dispensers, we hold a minor celebration to celebrate the day's achievements.

Feels good, getting off the console for a day.

At the start of Illyria's prolonged dusk, I return to my hab. For a long time, I regard the Show-Me, knowing I shouldn't go near. I really shouldn't. How much would a quick peek hurt, though? Swiftly I rationalize the impulse to do something I shouldn't into something I must: didn't Jerzemy say we were going to confab in after his meeting? No harm in checking in early. I could always switch off the console if I need.

Deep down, I'm fooling myself. Those justifications go down so smoothly, though.

With an electric thrill, I flip the switches.

Benny stands alone in Jerzemy's hab aboard the orbital. He's wearing the fanciest of his Rangers spokesperson jumpsuits: a red-and-white number sporting white fringe on the sleeves and side seams of the legs. I remember him commissioning it, the week he landed us Rancho Buck's. If it were zipped up, it would show the company's Stetson logo on his back in gleaming white, accented with gem-like lozenges to catch the spotlights. Tonight, though, Benny is unbuttoned to the navel. The upper half hangs from his waist to his ankles. Though the suit's designed to be worn with cowboy boots for the cameras, at the moment, he's barefoot. Both his hands wrestle with weight sticks.

The boy executes several curls, turned two-thirds away from Jerzemy's Show-Me. On my displays, I flick up new frames focused on and zoomed in upon parts of his body. Those round shoulders, glistening with exertion. The bulging biceps. The forearms, thicker and stronger than when I'd met him on Deimos. His hair, glistening in the light. That ass, pert and round. In mere moments, I have a dozen, two dozen views of him at various focal lengths; I'm surrounded by moving portraits of the Benny I cannot have.

His weight sticks are the thirty-centimeter variety, light as a dowel in storage, but interfaced with the orbital's grav generators to increase relative drag as needed. I drink in his features across my displays as he leans forward to adjust the sticks' downward pull with a swipe of his finger.

Why have I not noticed how much more of a man he's become? Hard to point out the differences, but there's a leanness in his face, a new level of definition. He exercises muscles that weren't at all there on Deimos. His beard used to strike me as youthful scruff, but now, filled in and thick, it accents his essential masculinity. I even think I can detect a gray hair or two among the gold. Pandemics do that.

I watch as he presses out his repetitions, then through another set. All the while, he whispers to himself. Lips working as he stares blankly ahead, again and again he lifts the weights with perfect form, then returns them to his narrow waist. Only when he turns off the sticks and tosses them aside is he finally at an angle for the mics to pick up, "...citizen leaders of the United Settlement, I am happy to present today..."

He's rehearsing a speech.

Though finished with his workout, he continues strolling around the room, grabbing a hand towel to mop himself off as he continues repeating the tricker parts of an upcoming presentation. "...we'll be ready to hit the ground running for the planet's very first...no, we'll be *primed* to hit the ground running..." He raises his arms one after the other, pointing to the ceiling while he wipes off his upper arms and lightly hairy pits. Then he dances back and forth, stretching those rangy muscles overhead to mop off his back. "...ready to *inaugurate* the planet's..."

Again, I am taken aback by his beauty. He begins pacing back and forth; the many close-ups on my Show-Me focus on his pecs, his flat stomach. When he tweaks at one flat pink disc of a nipple, I let out a sigh. My fingers undo the top snap on my own suit, then another. I'm exposed down to the fly before I can stop myself. Unlike Benny, I'm wearing a lightweight tank beneath— otherwise, my body hair snags against the suit's rough interior.

I should not be watching him.

I dismiss the thought the moment it pops into my head. Beautiful things are made to be enjoyed, and surely no one enjoys Benny more than I. He'd hate me spying—but at the same time, isn't it a form of flattery, taking such pleasure in his appearance, no matter how forbidden? He is finer than every block of marble, lost or preserved, sculpted into classical perfection. Though no longer mine, he's more precious than all the fine paintings in any museum. With supreme self-unconsciousness, he finishes swabbing the towel over his abs, then tosses it into the sonic Clean-Me's bin. I watch every graceful motion, rapt as I might be watching any master at his canvas.

"...ready to inaugurate *any* planet's first partnership with a leading corporate...oh, fuck it."

Without warning, he thrusts his hand down his pants. I let out the slightest of gasps.

Boardroom Benny transforms into Horndog Benny with the mercurial swiftness of an adolescent. I think he's still mouthing board-friendly platitudes when he reaches down to haul out the goods. His fly buttons loosen with an audible pop; I gape at the sight of his shaft in his right fist while his nuts drape over the taut red fabric below.

My frames on the displays autofocus all at once, juddering to keep up as he flops down on the bottom edge of Jerzemy's bed. His legs spread wide. I watch the top of his head as he ogles his hardening dick. A strand of spit descends, snapping halfway between his mouth and his target. Benny flicks out his tongue to gather the surplus that still lingers upon his lips. Then, eyes closed, his head lolls back as he rubs his free hand over his naked chest. Again, he tweaks a nipple, but this time with purpose: he tugs and squeezes for the sensations it arouses as his hand begins to fly up and down over the length of his meat.

Benny's dick isn't enormous, but it's pretty. His pubes are blond and thin enough that from a distance, they're almost invisible, giving the impression of depilated balls surrounded by little more than a flaxen fuzz. Erect, his cock projects straight forward but scoops up in a curve, like the stout pistil of a peace lily at proud attention. My displays magnify every breath-taking detail. The fleshy pink head, shiny with saliva. The anxious clench of his fist. The croak of his respiration as it grows more ragged. Another groan, like a strain of song, as he gives his nipple a further savage twist.

I shove my own hand down my shorts to grab at my cock. It feels right, gripping myself tightly in my fist as I watch my ex pleasure himself. With the frames zoomed in, I imagine myself close, thrilling to the heat of his skin, murmuring mixed encouragement and admiration into his ear. I'd tell him how beautiful he is, how proud he makes me. I should be there. Benny should be with me still. The things I would do for him...

Benny collapses back upon the mattress. I observe in awe as he shoves his middle finger deep in his mouth. Once it's wet, he stuffs his hand inside the open jumpsuit and probes for his ass. My own hole twitches in sympathy as I let loose a massive, guttural lament.

The sound has barely faded when the boy stops what he's doing and wrenches himself to a sitting position. Hands hiding his cock, his head whips in every direction. "Who's there?"

Oh, shit. Jerzemy didn't merely leave on his imager. My sound feed must be live. Maybe the display, too.

By the time I consider what to do, I've already done it. My back slams against the wall next to the console case, where I've sprung out of fear and instinct. I know at least I'm out of my imager's line of sight. As quickly as humanly possible, my fingers race to snap up my jumpsuit. So loud is my heart's thunder that if Benny says anything, I don't hear it over the mortified rush of blood in my ears.

I fret he'll see the seat of my console chair spinning around in place, launched into motion by my quick self-ejection. Why won't it stop spinning? For the love of gods, stop... This is the second time I've nearly been caught in my voyeurism. There won't be a third. Then and there, I make a vow to myself: if I get out of this situation, I'll make amends to Benny.

"Who's there?" I hear coming from the Show-Me.

I cannot simply fly over and shut everything down. To save face—his and mine—I grab what's nearby while I feign an imaginary conversation with an invisible guest. "Yeah, I don't think it'll be any problem. I'll pull up the statistics and see what the projections say." My breath is ragged. Am I too loud? I feel as if I'm talking too loudly. I wait an appropriate amount of time for a response. "All right, Jerry. Okay. Yeah, come back later, and we can figure it out."

By this time, I judge it safe to step back into view. Brandishing a data slate and, for some unknown reason, a wastebasket I snatched when I hit the wall, I stride back toward the console and assume my seat, waving off a Jerry who was never there.

Benny has his face pressed to Jerzemy's Show-Me, trying to see who's on the other side. So close is he to the imager that he's basically a convex forehead with eyes. He backs away once I swivel toward the display. My brain registers that I look ridiculous with the wastebasket in my lap, but it conceals the erection in my suit that hasn't yet gone down. "Hey there, Benny," I say, willing myself to appear calm. Friendly. Casual. The kind of guy who doesn't spend all his time spying on people's masturbation sessions like a damned pervert. "Nice to see you."

"Oh, fuck," he spits, not even bothering to disguise his utter loathing. "It's *you*."

Those words, dripping with contempt and disgust, hit like a wet slap to the face. Benny's usually sweet face contorts with disgust. "What the *fuck*."

Exactly once before has he been so angry. The last time I saw him, in fact. When we broke up for good.

It was the day before the drop-down to the planet, the day I visited the orbital's Biotech Lab for the last time, to create Jerzemy. The geneticists there already had a basic dupe template for my S-class clone's physical data from when I'd produced the two A-class Jerrys. Replicating a mental pattern, though, would take hours.

Benny didn't want me to do it.

The night before, he'd begged me to rethink the decision. Deep down, I understood how disturbing it had to be for him; he'd spent an entire week producing smiling feeds for the sponsor and stockholders that featured three dozen clones with my face loading up the drop ship. That's a lot of mes for a boyfriend to cope with. Yet I couldn't fathom why he pushed back so hard at the prospect of the final S-class duplication.

"It's unnatural," he had told me, face screwed up, much as it is now. "You've been duplicated enough."

I explained for what had to be the dozenth time

that there was no way around it. I'd lost most of my crew to the second pandemic. The handful remaining had scampered back to their homes. I alone couldn't perform the work of forty-four personnel. Forty-four Jeremys would. If United Settlements couldn't recruit that many scientists and technicians with my level of expertise—and after the second depopulation in twenty years, they could not—the only alternative was to manufacture forty Jers, two Jerrys, and a Jerzemy to work with me, each with my education and varying degrees of my skills.

None of my clones were created out of ego. Only dire necessity.

Benny and I had fought that last night before the final replication, long and loud. With shame I still remember what I said the next morning, before heading to the lab: *Not a word more about it. You're not slinging boba whiskey to grimy ore diggers here. Get over your backwater prejudices and do your fucking job.* Those words don't even sound like mine. I can't imagine them leaving my mouth.

Somehow, they did. The memory disgraces me.

Duping the Jerrys weeks before had been child's play, after the techs scanned my physical matrix. While strapped to a table at a sixty-degree incline, my head tightly caged so it wouldn't move, the techs mapped my neural connections while I read aloud from trade journals and textbooks. From time to time, the words would disappear, and puzzles would flash on a screen in front of me.

The Jerrys inherited slightly less than half of my neural matrix, as they'd pointed out the other night. An S-class clone would receive ninety-eight percent. It's a wildly expensive dupe, solely made in extreme circumstances. Yet the higher-ups at U.S. had decided the Illyria project was vital enough to budget for one. I'd concurred, much to Benny's dismay.

Perhaps he'd resented the responsibility I would owe to my S-class clone. The Jerrys would have a path to U.S. citizenship after a decade of service, including the right to a reproductive license if they chose. The Jers would receive neither of those—for now, anyway. Clone rights groups are all over the C-class disparity.

An S-class, though, gains immediate citizenship. All rights, privileges, and duties. In the event of his original's demise, he inherits the original's physical and intellectual property unless the clone specifically waives the right. My S-class would have no less authority than I over the Illyria project. Benny might even have to follow the clone's orders as if they were my own.

I can see how that would rankle.

But there I was, once again strapped and caged in the lab, tilted so that all I could see was the gentle light of the Show-Me screen above. This time, the duplication took over twelve hours. The techs started me with nursery rhymes and children's songs, then on to photos I'd accumulated through the years, which I'd view and narrate as their neuron tracers recorded and the molecular replicator buzzed away. There were more technical journals and multiple calculus problems and geometric proofs to solve.

And through it all, they made me read aloud the entirety of *Twelfth Night*. I am no scholar of ancient texts; some prankster in the lab must have made this selection because it takes place upon the shores of mythical Illyria, the same name as the planet we orbited. I stumbled from *If music be the food of love, play on,* through the unfamiliar words and puns and all the silly plot twists involving identical twins as best I could, sometimes switching out for more equations, until at least I reached the final *hey-ho, the wind and the rain* that finishes the play.

Shakespeare had a hand in naming this potential settlement site. *Journeys end in lovers meeting,* said some damned fool in the play. The phrase stuck in my brain; I used it when we encountered this biome.

After the replication's first few minutes, words lost their meaning. Mathematics became nonsense, though I eked out solutions. Visions of Benny's warped anger haunted every moment of the torture. Finally, though, it was over.

I remember being set free from the replicator and helped to stand on legs that seemed more viscous than solid. I was thirsty. My throat ached. My stomach growled. My head spun like it had been struck with a hammer. I was too dazed to fully register the sight of my clone being assisted to his feet across the room. I only had eyes for Benny, dressed in loose blue scrubs, consulting with the head lab technician.

Benny. My beautiful boy. The argument of the previous night forgotten, I'd stumbled toward him with open arms and light in my eyes.

He had backed away, repulsed. "Keep away from me. You...*monster*."

"Benny?" My first word, after rising.

He'd worn the same expression then as now. Twisted. Enraged. Disgusted. "Don't ever come near me again!" He spat the words like hot metal from a rivet gun. "I said, *keep away*."

A tech intervened and led me off before I could respond. I left for Illyria the next morning.

In his hab aboard the orbital, Benny has managed to pull his suit up over his shoulders and onto his arms. It remains undone in front, though. I politely avert my eyes. "Sorry. I was in the middle of a consultation down here. Did you need something?"

"Did I—!" He looks as if he's about to start frothing at the mouth but manages to calm himself down enough to snap, "What did you see?"

"What did I see when?" My lies are becoming even more practiced. "Didn't you open this feed?" He looks from my face to the wastebasket I'm clutching with both arms, uncertain of what to make of either. "While I've got you, is Jerzemy around?"

My timing must have been impeccable because Benny spins at the sound of his outer bulkhead being wrenched open. "I'll get him," he says, not without suspicion.

Whew. With my hard cock mostly deflated, I release my grip on the basket. On the bottom corner of the center display, in the frame showing my broadcast, I notice that I've missed a fastener and done up my jumpsuit crooked. Shit. I leap up, turn around, and manage to get every snap in its proper place by the time Jerzemy enters the hab. Once again at the console, I'm laid back, casual, and looking over the data slate while I listen to snatched phrases of their murmured conversation.

"Did you talk to him? What exactly were you two doing?" This, from Jerzemy to Benny, looking at the boy's wide-open jumpsuit with misgiving.

"Nothing. I didn't know the console was on! I was working out."

"Quiet, now." I ignore them until Jerzemy leans in and asks, "What do you need, Jeremy?"

Do I feel a stab of satisfaction, knowing I've kindled a squabble? Absolutely! Without a doubt. Not a trace of that shows, though, as smoothly I say, "Oh, just wondering how the committee went."

"Fine. Nothing big. We can talk about it tomorrow."

I nod and make an ostentatious show of yawning. "Night, then."

No farewell from my clone. Jerzemy reaches out and flips a single switch, turning off his own displays. As always, I hear and see the pair of them perfectly well. "You weren't up to anything, were you?"

"No!" Benny's fibbing. "I was getting in some curls, practicing my speech. You left the Show-Me on. I heard him talking to someone and went to see. That's all."

Jerzemy assesses, hands on his hips. Like me, he wears an unbranded jumpsuit in the dark blue and orange of the United Settlements. "We both know you like to show off." I can't tell if he's teasing or not. "Maybe you wanted to turn him on."

"Not at all." Benny's voice is practically a purr. He removes one arm from his suit, then the other. The heavy fringed fabric falls to the floor around the boy's ankles. "I only show off for you."

When I catch myself leaning forward to see what happens next, I remember my vow. Shaking my head, I disconnect all the feeds.

Benny's anger makes sense. I'd been the one to push him to the brink. I'd urged him to abandon friends and family to travel to my side, and he'd ended up in isolation for two long years. On the orbital, I'd thought of him as an ornamental appendage until he displayed his remarkable skills in negotiation. Even after, I'd ignored his sacrifices yet taken his gifts like a selfish child, without thanks. Then, I insisted on an S-class clone who would give him the same treatment.

No wonder he'd seethed at me.

I'm still sitting in silence a little while later when the display gently announces an incoming feed request from Logistics. Bald Jerry's image fills the screen. His handlebar mustache oscillates concern. "Jeremy, you there?"

"Where are you?" He's not in his hab. It's too dark. The acoustics aren't right.

"Had to take a sled out to the skimmer. Those damned brakes failed again. There was a minor accident."

That's not good—not late at night, out in unfamiliar territory. "Anyone hurt?"

"Nah. The skimmer got a little banged up when it

slammed against one of those limestone cliffs along the shore. You know the ones?" I do, but before I can say so, he continues. "Anyway, we found the weirdest thing."

"What is?"

"The collision shattered a thin outer layer of the stone, and...well. Let me show you."

There's a moment of confusion as Bald Jerry takes both a high-powered torch and portable imager from the sled and steps outside. I see first the pebbly beach underfoot, then some uncertainty as the light dances across the thirty-foot cliffs that help form a natural bay upon the massive lake. "I thought it was over here," says Bald Jerry, off-imager.

"No, further that way. There." That's Jerry, speaking from the Logistics hab.

"Yep. Got it." Bald Jerry shines the light onto the cliff and holds it steady. "Probably more visible in certain lights, but...do you see along this rock face? On the bottom, there's an almost oval horizontal sedimentary deposit of reddish silicate. And then on top of it, much taller and narrower, a vertical deposit, kind of oblong? It looks like..."

"I'll be damned," I say, astonished. "It almost looks exactly like the Rancho Buck's cowboy hat."

"Yeah," say the Jerrys in chorus. "Like the Rancho Buck's cowboy hat."

"If you squint," Bald Jerry adds.

I sit back in my chair and think. This project owes Benny. I owe Benny. I'll begin repaying him now.

❧ 6 ❧

The Convocation at Journey's End, as it would come to be known, takes place two days later. The entire family of Jeremy clones attend in our official role as Illyria's Planetary Preparation Rangers Co-sponsored by United Settlements Conservation Corps and Rancho Buck's Mighty Roast Beef Sandwiches. (It's still a mouthful.) Jerzemy and a handful of board members from the orbital touch down on a drop ship a few hours before the ceremony.

The Convocation is entirely Benny's responsibility. For two days, he's in his element, commanding his small team to stage the scene as grandly as our primitive conditions can accommodate. I stay out of his way, not once showing my face or intruding. We've barely enough outdoor respirators to go around for the scientific crew, so I occupy myself with replicating more for our guests.

Benny quickly devises a strategy. He envisions the event not merely as a christening for the forward station the clones and I have occupied for several months, but as a tribute to United Settlements lives lost during the second pandemic—a sure-fire way to get eyes on an otherwise dull formality. The inspiration elevates the ceremony into Benny's triumph. For centuries, every classroom Teach-Me will show the students of Illyria details of that evening, the night their planet was christened.

The feed goes live via tight-beam broadcast to neighboring systems shortly before one of Illyria's deep pink sunsets, as the red-orange glow of a giant bonfire on the beach catches the reflective silicate upon the thirty-foot rock face. The lights make the primitive Rancho Buck's logo sparkle. Clones in their branded jumpsuits and headgear sit and stand around the big fire, their silhouettes giving viewers an unforgettable image: ranch hands on the vista of the galaxy's newest and most unspoiled frontier, gathering at nightfall to pay tribute to their deceased comrades.

Benny acts as host throughout, introducing the speakers one by one. Bigwigs orate and speechify. A Rancho Buck's freight operator who happened to be making a delivery to the orbital is diverted from his duties, dropped planetside, and pressed into representing the sponsor. With unexpected charm and self-effacement, he delivers a speech pre-written by Benny on humankind's expansion to brave new worlds. At its conclusion, he requests a moment of silence to pay respect to the dead.

After the long hush, Benny steps to the podium and intones, "Thank you all for coming."

The ceremony is clearly over. And yet, seeing my Benny fringed and handsome, so clearly in his element, I feel compelled to add one finishing touch to the special night. I step forward and let my voice ring out.

Oh, give me a home...

It's an old, old tune, but familiar enough that everyone recognizes both lyrics and melody. The two Jerrys add their voices to mine, Bald Jerry in an upper harmony.

Where the buffalo roam...

By the third and fourth lines, all the Jers have

thrown their strong voices into the mix. My ears note how remarkably similar we all sound, singing in unrehearsed four- and six-part harmony. One vocalist, dubbed multiple times to approximate dozens. Our tempo is unhurried; our tone elegiac. We even breathe as one at the same spots.

And the skies are not cloudy all day.

The song concludes. The world falls silent. On the edited feed, which I'll view much later, it will be at this point that Benny has arranged for the Rancho Buck's Stetson Logo to fade in onscreen over its appropriate position on the limestone's face. Those of us present don't see the effect, of course. We stand with Stetsons to our chests, silent and still.

The event is actually pretty damned tasteful. It goes viral in a way no one could predict. Every news outlet carries footage. Reaction feeds flood social media. Not even an hour passes before tens of thousands of young folk anxious to serve on the new frontier planet barrage U.S. recruitment offices with applications. It will be a decade before Illyria is ready for settlement—but once it is, there will be more colonists competing for berths than transport ships to accommodate them.

All thanks to Benny.

Late that night, after the bonfire dies and most of our guests have returned to the orbital, I'm in my hab bed watching a replay of the feed on my slate. In the bottom right corner, the viewing numbers reel upward and upward. Good. I'm happy to see it.

Then I hear a rap at my door.

We don't maintain a pressurized atmosphere down here. Planetside, we've no need for deep space fail-safes like bulkheads. Our habs use simple doors that we tend to leave unlocked or even open, since we're forty-four men who share the same genetic imprint, and none of us have shown tendencies of thieving. My hab door stands ajar. Beneath the sheets, I'm naked. My shorts lie at the bed's foot, out of reach. I doubt one of the Jerrys or Jers would come calling; they'd be more inclined to barge right in. "Um, someone there?" I call out.

The door swings in slightly. A rumpled confusion of dense blond curls pokes around. "Oh," says Benny when he sees me with the bedclothes pulled to my naked chest. "I didn't—sorry."

My heart automatically thuds at the sight of his handsome bearded face, but I clear my throat and feign calm. "We made up a hab for you." *And for Jerzemy*, I leave unspoken. "Around the corner and three doors down." Bald Jerry cleaned out his quarters to accommodate them.

"Yeah, I...I know." A little more of Benny sidles into the room. He's shed his fringed uniform and only wears the lined white undergarments designed for beneath—a one-piece resembling a V-necked tee and mid-thigh boxer briefs, fastened by a PressTite strip down the center. Basically, a practical, short update on the ancient Union suit. His feet are bare despite these modular floors usually being chilly. "The room's fine, thank you. I couldn't sleep. It's just that..." As he looks around, my mind races for explanations to his unexpected appearance. "This looks a lot like Jerzemy's hab. Up..." He gestures skyward.

I could point out that there is not really a lot of variation in United Settlements standard domestic/work habs, but I nod vaguely and keep my tone brisk and professional. Pointed, too. "Is there anything you need? Did we forget something? For your guest hab? Down the hall?" I start sliding out from beneath the covers, then remember my state of nudity. Instead, I clutch them closer.

Benny's too fair-skinned to hide more heated emotions. His face reddens as he blurts out a single word: "Why?"

Why? Why what? I shake my head. Why did we

break up? Why did we argue? Why did I go through with the S-class clone? "I don't…"

"Why did you do this?" Now, he gestures westward toward Journey's End. "Did you, I don't know, *do* something to that cliff to entice me down here?"

There's an insinuation in his words I dislike. "Absolutely not! I'll sled you out to the skimmer and you can check its logs if you doubt me. The brakes were erratic all week. There was an accident. A layer of limestone chipped off. I wasn't even present." Remembering I'd been spying on him during the accident sets my own cheeks into a deep flush. "What lay beneath was happenstance."

"Quite a happenstance."

"I thought I was being helpful when I suggested you check it out." Are we arguing again?

"You were helpful. I'm—I'm sorry." He steps all the way into the room, closes the door, and leans against it like a chastened adolescent. "It was…" He averts his eyes to utter the words that follow. "…very nice of you."

His thanks feels backhanded, but I accept it with a nod. "That formation's not going to last forever. Natural erosion…particularly in a soft stone…"

"Yeah."

"Get your media while you can." He nods at my advice in a distracted manner. Though he stares at the floor, from time to time, I catch his eyes darting my way. Is it because I'm gripping my sheets like a timid virgin on her wedding night? I force myself to relax. "Um, if there's anything else…"

"I am uncomfortably aware I've been a total asshole to you." He blurts the words all at once. "I've been an asshole since the start. Then you have the nerve to turn around and hand me a win so huge that—and I *know* it will, and that's why it makes me so mad—so huge that it cements my legacy. Or something like that. It's just a weird thing for you to do!"

I'm confused. What he's saying sounds almost like gratitude, yet he pitches the words with such belligerence that all I can reply is, "I'm...sorry?"

"No. Shit." He waves his hands and tries again, this time stomping from the doorway to perch on the foot of my bed. "Everything's coming out wrong." His eyes close. "What I want to say is: thank you."

"You're welcome." I sound grave. Having him so close, though—almost at arm's length—and knowing he's not mine makes my heart painful and leaden.

"I want to know why."

My jaw tightens. Tears prickle behind my eyes, but I won't allow them to penetrate my mask of calm. "I did it because...you're my Benny. And despite everything...I will always..." The lump in my throat prevents me from saying what I want. "Because you're my Benny."

Benny cocks his head. In an incredibly soft voice, he says, "But I'm *not* your Benny."

I suck in my lips to stop them quivering. When my emotions are under control, I admit, "You have no idea how deeply I regret that."

Somewhere down the corridor, a door slams, and one Jer calls out a goodnight to another. Then silence. Benny regards me for a long moment. He toys with the bed's blanket all the while. "Were you watching me the other night?"

"Yes. But not for very long." Now is my chance to come clean. "It was unforgivable, and I truly apologize..."

He stops me. "Did you like what you saw?"

This isn't the question I expect. After I clear my throat, I admit, "Yes. So much."

He hesitates a moment. Our eyes meet. Exactly like the other night, he mutters, "Fuck it."

I find myself propelled backward, deep into the pillow, as, with one feline leap, the boy lands atop me. His mouth connects against mine with such violence that he smashes my upper lip. I don't care. It's the sweetest pain. Benny's feet kick at my coverings, sending them flying. His knees part my thighs as he presses all his weight into me. His strong arms squeeze so tightly that my ribs creak. The friction of my naked skin against his undergarments makes me harden instantly; I feel his cock grinding against my own through a layer of thermal lining.

I consider pinching myself to make certain I'm not dreaming. Would I want to awaken if I were? "Benny," I breathe, seizing the sides of his head. "Don't do this because of the..."

"I do what I want." His eyes bore into mine with the intensity of a mining laser. I'm still cradling his skull as he begins ripping open the PressTite seam running down his truncated Union suit. "I want this. I want you." I let go as he jumps from the bed onto the floor. His titanium-hard cock points at me like an accusation, once he shimmies from his garments. "I want you in me." He spits on his hand, squats slightly, and rubs it on his hole. Then he pounces again, landing on the bed with force enough to send me flying. "And you're going to fuck me tonight. Before I go back to the orbital."

He's spitting in his hand again and grabbing for my meat, preparing to mount me. I capture his wrist. "No," I tell him. "Not like that." His nostrils flare at being denied his prize. I sit up and bring myself close. "If all I get is this one last chance with you, we do it my way."

My lips travel over his face, planting soft kisses on his cheeks, his chin, the closed lids of his eyes, his forehead. At last, they linger upon his mouth. He tolerates the gentleness for a moment, then attempts to escalate by pulling me hard against him. I resist.

Perhaps Jerzemy prefers it rough, but not I. Not tonight. "Lie back," I tell him. We maintain eye contact as he concedes among the pillows. I shift my feet onto the floor. "Turn over." I rotate my index finger to indicate he should lie face down.

"What are you going to do?"

I let his question linger as I cross the hab to make sure the door is latched. I activate the lock. "Do what I say, and you'll see."

There's a bit of apprehension in his shoulders as he pulls his chest up onto the pillows. His head hangs over their edge, face down. At the bottom of the bed, I hover tall and allow my eyes to feast upon the sight. His ass, like ample scoops of creamy melon, smooth and appetizing. The dip of his back between the peak of his buttocks and his broad, strong shoulders. His creamy thighs, spread in invitation. I swallow, hardening from the little gasp he lets out when I seize an ankle in each hand to widen his legs further. "Please," he whispers.

Those spread legs are my runway; I pilot my body between them and coast up the mattress to my final destination. The boy jumps when I grab hold of his cheeks and pull them apart. My tongue darts into the exposed crevice to lap at his pucker. I'm aware he's making feral noises, but my own ears are too full of the sound of my blood dancing to the cadence of my heart.

He tastes good. He's not freshly sonicked, but neither is he raunchy. His skin carries the natural perfume of a man at the end of a long day's work. Benny's smell. I intend to relish it. Deeply, I inhale, savoring the mingled scent of sweat and musk, the faded odor of the Clean-Me's sanitizers, a slight tang from beneath his fuzzy balls. His hole itself tastes slightly metallic, as if I've licked an iron bar. Still, it's warm and pliable to my lips. I flatten my tongue as wide as I can and lap at his entry.

"Oh, my," is all he can say. Then, in softer tones, "Please!"

In my hands, Benny oscillates between tension and relaxation. Tenses when my tongue makes its slow and unrelenting journey from taint to crack. Relaxes when I withdraw and breathe onto the wet skin. Tenses again when I gnaw on his most sensitive spot; relaxes when I back down to admire my handiwork. One moment, he's clawing his curled toes into the mattress. The next, his limbs slacken to become biddable to my touch.

"You are so beautiful," I whisper. My lips graze the rise and sweet decline of his ass, the small of his back, the spot between his shoulder blades. "Every centimeter." I raise his left arm high and bury my face in his pit, again sniffing until my lungs are full of him. Here, he smells of spice, exotic and precious. "Every spot."

This version of Benny is as far as can be from the sexual aggressor prepared for onslaught minutes ago. He's tractable and passive, a sleepy lad willing to be trundled to bed. Eyes lidded, he breathes, "Jeremy..."

I thrill to hear my name upon those pretty lips.

"Sshh." I roll him onto his stomach and pull myself up so that my mouth skims close to his ear. My fat cock fills the space between his thighs, making him gasp and grind upward with his hips. "Let me show you exactly how beautiful." Without protest, he surrenders completely.

For a long and satisfying time, I indulge myself on his ass, tasting it, chewing at it, teasing it with the stubble on my chin. Periodically, my hands will scoop beneath his thighs to draw him more firmly onto my face; at other times, I part his cheeks and expose his pink pucker to the cool hab air. I grunt like a pig hunting for truffles among the Arcturan hickories. He, in turn, gasps and sighs with my every new discovery.

"Turn over." He does so without protest, regarding me with a liquid gaze. I prop myself on my elbows and simply take my time to survey the boy. Tonight may be my one chance. I intend to be greedy while I may. In my foreground vibrates his cock, keeping time with his heartbeat and the rapid rise and fall of his chest. Beyond that, the smooth valleys and plains that are his abs, then the gentle hillocks of his pectorals. I, who have evaluated more planets than most men, would be content to spend a lifetime confined to this landscape before me.

His laughter is helpless. Vulnerable. "You make me feel shy."

"Why?"

"I..." His hands attempt to cover his arousal. I shake my head and swat them away. I am too entranced with this view to cede it so quickly. "Jerz never looks at me like you do."

The sound of my rival's name triggers my most unsportsmanlike urges. "You're not in Jerzemy's bed tonight," I remind him, trying not to gloat.

"No," he says with the slightest of half-smiles, as if grateful to be reminded.

"Whose cock is this?" I pull myself closer to wrap his fingers around me. I'm rigid. Swollen. Beneath the foreskin that's half retracted, the glans glows an angry scarlet.

One hand squeezes. The other joins it to tug at my balls. "Yours," he breathes.

This time, I make audible my displeasure. "Whose?"

"This is Jeremy's cock." His voice is meek.

"That's right. Why don't you look it over? Nice and close."

We swap places so that I'm leaning against the pillows while he hovers near my hips. My flesh jerks and jumps in his palms as he inspects the hefty piece. His warm breath singes my skin. "It's exactly like his. Every vein. Every mark. But it belongs to you."

The excitement in his eyes betrays him: I can tell he's about to attempt something hasty. Something hungry. The moment his mouth opens, before he can dive, I shake my head. "Gently," I chide. "Just kiss it." He's unused to restraint. His thick locks are the ideal grip for my left hand, however. A fistful of gold, so I can lead his pouty lips to the tip of my dick and ensure they go no further. "Kiss it."

Benny licks his lips and applies the tenderest of pecks to—well, my pecker. Of its own volition, my stiff meat jerks and trembles at his touch, demanding more. I guide him a little lower so he can apply another smooch further down. I angle his head to one side, then the other. Throughout the exercise, he gazes unwaveringly to judge my reaction. When I smile and nod, letting him know how much he pleases me, I'm rewarded by the admiration in his eyes.

"You're a beautiful boy," I remind him. "You're a good boy, too."

He licks his lips and swallows. "Thank you. Thank you, sir. I want to be good. Thank you." Each expression of gratitude grows fainter as I maneuver him toward my scrotum. Unlike Benny, I'm a hairy beast. My nuts are no exception. I've never once depilated; hair down there grows thick and dense, like bamboo. But he sighs with happiness to be of service, his nostrils huffing deeply of my scent. A lungful is almost a narcotic for him: his eyes close, and he mutely laps and worships the source of my seed. When I maneuver him onto his back and prop up his head with pillows, he's as pliant as plasticine.

"Open up," I say. He steels himself to comply.

Slowly, I enter him, centimeter by centimeter. His smooth hands clutch for my chest to run themselves through my fur. To me, all this body hair is an inconvenience. The stuff is always shedding all over the bathroom or getting caught in snaps and seams, pulling and tugging at the worst times. To Benny, it's an aphrodisiac. He caresses my pelt from clavicle to navel like he might a cat, sheerly for tactile joy. Every stroke multiplies the sensations I experience as slowly, ruthlessly, I invade his mouth.

Past the lips I push, my foreskin gently retracting at their delicious friction. The deeper I penetrate, the moister and hotter he seems. Soon, to both our delight, I'm knocking against his tonsils. And I'm only two-thirds of the way in. For a moment, he struggles, his mouth stretched to its limits. I look down, cup his cheek, and say, "Beautiful."

Then he relaxes and admits more.

I could shoot so easily from this attention. His baby blues gazing up at me. That expression of happiness mingled with an apprehension of what is yet to come. The sight of his own cock curving upright as he continues caressing the thick pelt covering my chest. The sloppy gargle of his choking and gulping.

Yet, I need more. Wet as his mouth is, and thought soft his velvety tongue, I require something wetter and tighter. "Get that cock slick," I murmur. His eyes widen. He knows what's coming.

Now, I allow him to become a little more gluttonous. His appetite inflames me. Every sound of struggle on my fat meat makes me more rigid. Though my hand rests on the back of his head, he requires no guidance. The boy stabs his throat onto my tool as deeply as he's able, making sure to soak it with saliva.

Once his spit drips from my nuts, with care, I settle him onto the mattress. I take a pillow, fold it in half, and, using his feet on my shoulders for leverage, wedge it beneath the small of his back. In my right hand, my cock is slimy from his sucking. Benny's feet fly high in the air; his knees close in on his chest as he rests his weight squarely on his muscular shoulders. I cannot resist a last taste. Eyes locked with his, I seize his cheeks and pull them to my face, lapping broad strokes over his hole. Gooseflesh covers his skin, fanning from his butt to his thighs, up his sides, across his chest. Both his chest and face redden, not merely from the upending of his circulatory system but from the moment's immensity: an immovable mouth has collided with an irresistible hole, pushing every law of physics past its breaking point.

"I want this," I growl as I gnaw on him once again. Beneath my lips, his hole twitches and blooms. "Let me inside."

He half-laughs, half-sobs. "I want you too. So bad."

"Yeah?" I'm cruel to deny him. But I like hearing the entreaties from his lips.

His head bangs the mattress. "I need you to ruin me. Punish that hole. Please. Ah!" While he's talking, I've grabbed his ankles with one big hand and hoisted them high. He resembles a young buck strung up and ready for the feast. Then I've stabbed the blunt head of my cock against him. I haven't penetrated, yet, but the surprise of it is enough to get a reaction.

"It might hurt." I both hope it will and won't.

Benny's nods become short and emphatic. "Make it hurt," he begs. "Wreck me with your cock. Jeremy's cock. Jeremy's cock should be inside me."

I can't help myself. Hearing my name on his lips drives me wild. No longer can I wait; I'm a breast-beating savage grappling with the urge to pillage and plunder what should be mine. I have dreamed of something sweeter with Benny, though, so it takes all my will to resist that bestial impulse. Drawing a deep breath, I say, "Hey." The word breaks the spell my dick has cast. "Look at me."

Eyes wide, he obeys.

"I'm going to slide this cock inside you. And you're going to love...every...bit." Already, I've started my invasion, a centimeter at a time. My lip curls at the sight of his silent gratitude. Then, the ridge of my mushroom head disappears inside. "If you're a good boy and make me happy, what do you think I'll do?"

He doesn't need the narration. He's fucked before. I enjoy spinning it out, though—giving him what he wants and needs in slow, measured doses while encouraging him to anticipate the rest. My tease succeeds: I witness his chest rise and fall as he begins panting more quickly. The further in I slide, the harder his own cock grows. I swat away his hand as he grabs for himself, though. "I hope you'll cum in me," he whispers, abashed at his overexcitement. "I want you to fuck me. Reward me with that load."

I nod. "If you're a very...very...good...boy." Between each of the last words, I push in a bit more. With his legs spread, I can reposition myself between his open thighs. From above, I look down. My lips are close enough to his that I feel his hot breath on my face. "Are you going to be a good boy, Benny?"

"Yes—oh *gods*." I've already foreseen his answer and shoved the rest of myself inside in one swift onslaught. His hole clutches tight from the shock of being so suddenly stretched. The reaction sends thrills up and down my spine. I barely can resist slamming into him. Yet I know I'm big. He needs time to adjust. Eventually, he loosens up. I meet with almost no resistance as I slowly begin sliding in and out. "I'll be a very good boy if you keep doing that." He delivers the promise with almost tearful sincerity.

This connection between us is galvanic. Elemental. Why are we no longer together, when our coupling feels so essential? The circuit completes when my mouth covers his, and, with eagerness, he accepts my tongue inside. With every thrust, his legs flail. Over time, as I continue grinding deep inside and my heavy balls slap loudly against his backside, they curl around my hips. Drawing me in. Holding me.

At first, I fuck to please him. My head hammers against the button of his prostate so relentlessly that all he can do is claw and thrash. As exquisite torture, I grind and mash my forest of pubes against his hole. I kiss him soft, then rough, to inflame our passion. "I need this," I growl in his ear. "I need you to open wide. Let me in." Harder I thrust, solely for the pleasure of hearing him whimper. "Let all this big dick in. Jeremy's dick. That's right." When, in one acrobatic swoop, he scoops the back of his knees with his elbows and draws them closer to his ears, I nod in approval. Then, I unleash the ultimate praise. "Good boy."

If I'd not already been all the way inside, those two words would have made his hungry butt suck me in like a black hole. "Thank you," he breathes. The smile he wears as he gazes up at me, I will forever remember. It makes me want to pound him harder.

So, I do.

I don't entirely understand what I feel as I plow away. Benny and I have fucked before. I have fond memories of nights on Deimos, banging away in my lodgings. I need only recall our reunion after the pandemic when two years of separation and longing had me balls-deep inside him for what felt like weeks on end.

Yet I don't remember these specific sensations: the ticklish pleasure of sheath sliding against chute, my balls demanding to release the building pressure, the scent of spit and precum heated by friction. I don't recall these little noises of pleasure issuing from deep in his gut, some produced by my substantial weight upon him, some kindled from his desire for harder and rougher treatment.

Why do I not remember these aspects of making love to Benny? Have I forgotten? Or has our long parting made tonight's experience all the sweeter?

No matter. Before, I might have been thinking of his pleasure. Now, my own takes precedence. Some invisible motor deep within drives me. I couldn't stop if I wanted to. My cock stabs at his guts as if it wants to disembowel the boy. His hands bang the mattress, sounding the surface like a bass drum. Whether he means to egg me on or urge me to slow down—I don't care. I intend to get what I want. In this very moment, that's Benny's hole.

I'm fucking Benny. I'm giving my boy the fuck of his life.

"Yes!" His words pierce the deafening roar of whatever demon possesses me. "Ruin that ass!"

"I'll ruin it for any other fucker after me," I vow through gritted teeth. "After this, every time this sweet little hole gets beat up, you'll wish it was my dick."

He grabs his own curved pistil and begins to stroke. "I'll wish it was Jeremy's dick. I love Jeremy's dick."

"Jeremy's dick," I repeat. That's when Jeremy's dick starts to blast.

I might have been a quiet shooter those times I spied upon Benny with my clone, but not tonight. Surely, the entire forward station overhears my roar of triumph and surprise. My spine arches. My head flies back. Every muscle tenses.

Beneath me, Benny urges me on. His fingers clutch at my hairy ass to pull me hard into him. He bucks and jerks, coaxing out every drop. "I feel it. I feel it!" he keeps saying. His amazement makes me open my eyes. I hadn't been aware I clenched them shut.

His spasmodic twitches aren't solely to milk me dry. He's using my dick to bring himself to climax. Deftly I take over for him, swabbing the fluid that drips from his hole onto my fingers and slapping the stuff onto his cock for lubrication. Beneath my fist, his dick swells hotter and thicker. Our eyes connect. I nod, letting him know the time has arrived. "Come for me."

"For Jeremy."

If only he knew how hope both thrives and dies when he speaks my name.

His orgasm is as intense as mine. Yet he's almost silent, heralding its approach with sighs and lips that work through mute prayers and promises. His load soaks my bed. From his nearly upside-down posture, semen sprays in every direction. Some marks his face; a good deal of it, warm and sticky, lands on his chest and the back of my hand that's planted to its side. My other fist is covered with the stuff as gradually I slow down my ministrations. Enough DNA splatters across my bedclothes to make an entire squadron of clones.

Panting and abashed, he looks at me with a laugh. "Oh, my."

It's so comically mild a statement after our profanity-ridden fuck—so Benny—that I grin in agreement. "Oh, my, indeed."

I sink down next to him and attempt to take him in my arms. He's not finished, though. While I stroke his hair, he curls into a ball upon his side, takes my still-swollen cock in his mouth, and gently cleans it off. A few times, when the buds on his tongue rasp against my unsheathed glans, I almost yelp. Mostly, though, I relish the sensation of his warm, wet mouth as it nurses at my softening shaft.

"Jeremy's cock," he mumbles through a mouthful. "I had Jeremy's cock in me."

"Yeah, well." I chuckle. "Jeremy's cock enjoyed it." Understatement, that.

"Just..." He snuggles close and rests his head upon my chest, still flipping my meat back and forth with his soft fingers. "Don't tell Jerzemy." The words sound uncomfortable in his mouth.

So. I'm to be his secret. A last forbidden tryst with the ex. With a heavy heart, I swallow my sorrow. Still, I pull him close, protecting him while I can. "I truly hope you don't regret what we..."

"Nooooo." He reassures me with a kiss to the cheek. "Not a regret in the world. Jerz and I have never been exclusive, but...I don't think he'd be super happy I wanted tonight of all nights with you." No. He wouldn't. Perhaps Benny sees the happiness he'd gifted me during the last hour evaporating before his eyes, because he sits up and cups my cheek. "Hey. You are an amazing lovemaker. Tender, passionate. Connected in a way I don't...you know. Usually get." He changes his train of thought. "Tell me. Was I—what I mean is, I wasn't your first. Right?"

"My first?" I fail to understand. Self-recrimination begins eating away at me. I'd not been the initiator of this encounter. Perhaps I should have resisted harder. "My first since I made planetfall, yes. My first in five months."

"So, your first." He shakes his head. "Wild. I wish I'd known."

I'm still confused. "That was the first sex I've had since we broke up, yes."

"Since we broke..." Perplexed, he shakes his head. "You and I didn't...Jeremy. We were never together. Wait—you know that, right?"

I think of Deimos, of that terrible boba whiskey. I think of his giddy joy on the Show-Me when I'd told him about the berth I'd purchased upon that tiny medical supply ship. I think of all the times we'd talked for hours from our respective isolations and how he'd flung himself at me aboard the orbital when, after two years, we'd reunited.

I think of how I rose from the replicator the night before I departed for Illyria. Of stumbling toward him. Of the first word I spoke: *Benny.*

"No. You and I were together." Forming tears blur the outline of his face. "We were boyfriends. We loved each other, Benny."

"Oh, no. No, no." With each denial, he peppers my cheek with a kiss. "Sweet man. How long have you thought—you actually believe Jerzemy is *your* clone. Don't you?"

"Jerzemy is my clone."

Rising from the replicator. Stumbling. *Benny.*

"No, Jeremy. He's not. You are his." The sound of

my name brings me back. "I am so sorry. Please forgive me. I've heard sometimes clones are confused when they're created, but I thought by now...Jerzemy is the original. You are his clone. I've always been with Jerzemy."

In space, when a ship's artificial gravity goes offline, there's no warning—only a cessation of a certain ever-present whine when the drives power down. Then, things gradually lift up and begin to float. People, slates, markers on desks, coffee freed from its cup. Everything not bolted down or held with magnets sets itself aloft gently and silently. Though I'm planetside, rules of gravity no longer seem to apply. Everything I thought I knew has come unmoored, and I with it. I am without weight, slowly lifting and wheeling around and around and around.

One small truth has upended my world.

"No." My protest is little more than a weak mew. I sense he's spoken honestly, but I cannot yet accept it. "That can't be. He's my..." Benny shakes his head. *No.* "Then what am I?"

I look to Benny for support. For encouragement. Everything is topsy-turvy, but he remains aground. "You spent the last hour showing me what you are." He holds tight onto my hand. "You're a sweet and thoughtful man. A gentle lover."

"I am...Dr. Jeremy Wollny. Scientist. Explorer. Citizen. True?" He nods, pity filling his eyes. "And you are saying..." I puzzle out the words before I utter them aloud. "I am the class S clone of Dr. Jerzemy Wollny. Created at unthinkable expense by the United Settlements to share in the responsibility of transforming the planet Illyria."

The wild shores of Illyria. *Journeys end in lovers meeting.*

"Yes." Benny presses hands upon my chest, anchoring me. As once more I descend to the planet, he is my gravity. "I'm Benny Dahl. I was an asshole to you, moments after you took your first breath. I regret..."

I stop him. Living upside-down for so long has left my head spinning. Being righted again unburdens me of old sins that never were mine. "You and I didn't fight the night before I went—before *he* went to be cloned. You fought with *him*."

"I was frightened. I don't know why."

"I never said those awful things to you."

"What awful...? You never said anything awful at all." I've confounded him with another man's memory.

"And tonight was—oh." Those sensations of making love. How unfamiliar they had seemed. "This really was my first time with someone. *My* first time."

"I thought you knew what you are." He's still apologizing. Though I attempt to cut him off, he needs to have his say. "If it's consolation, for a first-timer, you were good. Great, even. Almost better...you know." He bites down that thought and substitutes one more politic. "There really are differences between you two."

I gift him a smile.

What is Benny to this new me? So much more than a flash of spring sunshine on a cloudy day. More than a trick picked up on a mining moon, more than an Illyrian one-night stand. Benny is...Benny. He is his own creation. He's not my possession. Never was, never will be. He's the ideal impressed upon me by an overworked scientist lying upon a genetic replication table while solving math problems and reading Shakespeare.

The realization saddens me. But there's absolution in it, too.

"You are a beautiful and amazing young man." I feel...fine. I feel myself, perhaps for the first time. Sweet of him to worry for me. But that's Benny. I kiss his forehead. "Don't worry. I'm thankful for tonight."

The relief is writ plain across his face. "Truly?"

"Truly. Now, scoot."

I've tried to sound as light-hearted as possible, but I need time to myself. Time to think. He hesitates, however. "You're not going to do anything foolish?"

"Define foolish."

"I'm not leaving if you're not one hundred percent okay."

"One hundred...?" I share ninety-eight percent of Jerzemy Wollny's brain patterns and memories. That doesn't make me only ninety-eight percent of a person. "No. I'm complete."

"I won't leave if you'll be lonely."

This time, my laugh is genuine. I am Jeremy Wollny, scientist. I have been posted to the planet Illyria and assigned a crew entirely of my own genetic replications. Countless patterns, all of us cut from the same bolt of cloth.

I can never truly be lonely, for I am multitudes.

I'm amazed at what a single viral social media feed can accomplish that months of appeals, board meetings, and prospectuses cannot. Six months after the Convocation at Journey's End, my project's budget has doubled. United Settlements citizens speak with renewed excitement about expanding the galactic frontier. Orbital workers have shuttled up and down to install new modules on the forward base to house anticipated new personnel. They've added another mess hall, though it equally smells of roast beef and fryer oil. There's chatter about a second or even third skimmer to accelerate planetary seeding.

Furthermore, we've been awarded new Show-Mes. Voice-activated models with multiple imagers and displays that can fill a wall if necessary. The kind of Show-Mes one might find in a high-end emporium, rather than patched together from cannibalized discards.

Moments ago, three Jers installed mine, in fact—wheeling it on a pushcart straight from a drop ship that landed an hour ago. Now that it's connected to the power supply, I should be able to turn it on and...

The Show-Me whirrs to life with an electronic hum. Imagers read the room's dimensions and project displays above the console. It's fancy. So fancy. It might take a week to figure out what's what and where.

I'm absorbing myself in reconfiguring displays to suit my workflow when an incoming feed creates its own frame. "I'll accept," I tell the Show-Me, which obligingly enlarges and opens the request. I don't have to touch a thing!

"Jeremy. I hope you received my gift?"

His hair's trimmed and his face even leaner than before, but he's still the Benny that softens my heart whenever I see him. In the background of the orbital hab, I can spy Jerzemy working out with weight sticks. I can't help but smile, remembering the night of the Convocation. My first time. But I've learned how to play it cool and keep it casual where Benny's concerned. We both have.

"Heya. Yes, thanks. Wait. You sent something?" The new equipment hails from United Settlements and our sponsor, not from Benny. Unless he's speaking more broadly about bringing the project so much attention? "Are you talking about my new Show-Me? Because..."

Am I mistaken, or is he smirking? "No, Jeremy. I don't mean your new Show-Me. What I sent down obviously hasn't arrived. I'll let you go." He peers around before leaning in. Out of Jerzemy's earshot, he confides, "Our sponsor is fond of an old Earth saying: *you can lead a horse to water...*"

"But you can't make it drink?" I'm lost. Did he send me a horse? We don't have room for a horse.

"In this case, more like: *you can't force that horse to love you,*" Benny corrects. He wears a secret smile meant exclusively for the two of us. "Keep it in mind. But Jeremy —I think you could have a real shot."

"Knock-knock?"

I sigh at the interruption. The last thing I want in the middle of this baffling conversation is the latest round of dad jokes from the Jerrys. "Not now..." I bark as I wheel around to see who occupies the entry to my hab. Then, "Oh. My."

"Sorry to interrupt. Your door was open." A young man walks unevenly into my office. I recognize the gait. Space legs. This must be his first time planetside in a long spell. Maybe his first ever. He radiates nervousness.

My heart begins thudding even before I've assimilated the sight before me. A mop of curly blond hair. A short beard. Broad shoulders. Narrow waist. Baby blue eyes. I recognize that face.

I have loved that face.

"I'm Ben," says the boy.

My lips part, suddenly dry and uncooperative. I cannot speak. The newcomer wears the standard U.S.-issued jumpsuit issued to A-class clones. The resemblance is...well. Remarkable. I always thought Benny would end up making more money than he knew what to do with.

Mistaking my silence for doubt, the young man clears his throat. "I arrived on the drop ship, earlier? The orbital deployed me to assist you and the Rangers with P.R. This will be my first assignment, but if you need press releases, or promotional opportunities... that's why I'm here."

He's coltish in his awkwardness, and so, so eager to make a good impression. I must look like a foolish brute, standing stock still, jaw agape. I can't help staring, though. He looks exactly like Benny.

The boy pauses midway through his prepared introduction to echo me. "Have we met? I had an interview with Dr. Wollny on the orbital, of course. You two look exactly...sorry. That's a silly thing to say. Of course, you look...I know you're his...I'm one myself...I mean, I know who you are, but..." He cocks his head like a curious bird, stops his stammering, and returns my stare with his own. "Have we met before?"

It is time I assume command. "We have not. I'm Dr. Jeremy Wollny." I offer Ben a handshake. "Welcome to Journey's End."

I'll show the new recruit around in a moment, but first, I have to thank someone. When I turn, however, the bank of displays is dark.

Benny has turned off his Show-Me.

BILLY CLUB

BY FRANK SLATER

Wheels skidded across the wet street bringing the bike to a standstill perfectly aligned with the curb in front of the yellow sign of Hounds Liquor. Black leather knee-high boots slapped down into the filthy puddling water draining out of the clogged pipes by the shattered glass door of the shop. Across the street Alastair's eyes moved up from the boots to tight black pants with navy blue stripes running up the sides. They terminated at a thick black belt, complete with holster, cuffs, and all the regular accoutrements of police gear.

The fuzz entered the store before Alastair could catch a glance of his face. But he had a feeling that he knew the look. His walk was familiar. That firm and confident stride as he had cleared the curb and kicked the bike into a parked position, all with one seamless move. He'd probably only be in there for a few minutes, take the report and leave, since there wasn't really anything the cops could do about busted windows. This didn't give Alastair and Diego much time to do what they had come to do.

"You catch his badge number?" Alastair asked.

Diego gave him a funny look. "Are you kidding? He was only in sight for a second. That and with his back turned. Did you?" He shook his head to match his sarcasm.

"I didn't see shit. You go in there, bump into him or something. Get that number."

Diego kept on shaking his head. "You're fucking kidding, right? Make contact! You go in there and get it yourself."

"Shit, man. I'm the one that broke the glass door. You do something for a change. It's not like this is just for me. Get the fucking badge number." He socked Diego on the arm while saying this, signaling that he meant it. But Diego didn't budge. Wouldn't budge. He was as lazy as he was as he was unhelpful. But damn right he would want to get up on this once the action started.

They waited across the street trying to act like they belonged there, trying not to draw attention, but looking like the couple of criminal bums that they were. The minutes ticked away slowly and still the officer didn't come back out onto the street.

"What do you think he's doing in there? What's taking so long?" Diego asked, as if Alastair would know. As if he wasn't standing right next to him blind to what was happening in the liquor store. Alastair lit a smoke and said nothing. Didn't even look away from the shop and toward his accomplice.

They had the cop figured for a Billy, but which one, there was no way of saying without the badge number. They all looked identical. All had that firm ass in those tight pants. Were all almost unapproachable. That is, if you didn't know how to get their attention properly and what to do with it once you had it. Alastair knew. But he was a collector, unlike the sloppy Diego who would take whatever he could get, whenever he could get it. It was a miracle that things ever worked out for him at all, for he was almost never willing to put in any effort. He wasn't the hunter type, he was the get-by on the minimum type. A contrast to Alastair in almost every way.

Diego broke the silence, "You gonna go in there and get it?"

"Fuck no! That was supposed to be your job, fool." He spat out the last of his cigarette and pulled a pair of cheap, small binoculars from his back pocket. He knew Diego was going to be useless and he wasn't about to let the whole thing go to waste, not after risking his ass breaking the window in broad daylight. "Stand in front of me. Make sure no one is tripping on me out here 'birdwatching' in the middle of the city."

Diego took the cue and ambled forward while trying unsuccessfully to look natural.

"Not too much in front of me. I still need to be able to see him, and that badge. Get it together. Some partner you are."

A long string of unintelligible grumbles came from Diego, his usual way of arguing or dismissing, without actually articulating his anger or defiance. But he stooped a little, leaning up against a parked car to give Alastair a better vantage.

"Where is that guy? Is he ever coming out? Damn thing about these super cops, they're always trying to actually do their jobs. Worth it though, I suppose. Couldn't have made them so good out of one of those slouches. If they had, he'd probably just kick our asses and take off..." Alastair's words drifted off as he spotted the Billy start to head out, pause at the door to survey the damage, and turn to say one last thing to the store clerk.

"Turn around, you fucker." whispered Alastair.

Diego turned, "What's that? I didn't hear you."

"Shut up. You weren't supposed to. Just make sure that he doesn't see me yet. Look natural you bonehead."

Diego began to protest and then thought better of it. The cop finished whatever he was saying and walked back out to the sidewalk. He looked at his bike with pride and then up and down the street as if he might spot the culprit lurking around. And sure enough he was, just not on that side of the street.

Alastair brought the binoculars up to his face, both obscuring his mug and giving him a closer look at the Billy. And sure enough, he was a Billy. There was no denying that handsome, many of a kind, face. He was a model specimen. Perfect in nearly every way. And the uniform only added to his allure.

Alastair zeroed in on the badge and read the number out loud, "Number fifty-six. It's not him. But I never seen this one before. Don't have a notch for that number yet. But that badge sits nicely on him."

Billy #056 mounted his motorcycle and started to pump it into gear, the muscles of his arms bunching as he took control of the machine. The bike was loud, even over the sound of the thick traffic of the nearby freeway. He revved the engine several times and was about to pull out.

"Shit, he's going to get away. You idiot! You should have gone over there when I told you to."

Without waiting for a response Alastair pushed Diego out of the way and jaywalked across the street in a hurry. He wasn't about to let 056 get away that easily. Not after all it had taken to get him to show up in the first place. But him being on the bike already wasn't going to help, he could be up and out of there any second.

Picking up his pace Alastair ran in the direction of the cop, hoping to get in front of him before he had the chance to zoom away. An impatient driver nearly ran him down, eliciting a barrage of honks from the offender as the surrounding cars joined in. The racket didn't slow him down and he leapt in front of the bike, already panting from the short run. The Billy looked him up and down with that stiff cop scrutiny, inviting and deadly at the same time.

With his hands on his knees, halfway hunched over, Alastair took a second to catch his breath. 056 started to look more impatient than ever and began to palm his night stick while continuing to rev the bike.

"I saw the whole thing. He came out of there looking mad, smashed the glass, and took off down that way." He pointed to the west. "The guy ran that way. Must have been almost ten minutes ago."

The Billy looked at him incredulously and didn't budge. His demeanor made Alastair shake in his boots. Part authority, part danger, all man. His silence suggested that he would remain unmoved by a single eye-witness account.

"I swear. I can show you. He ran off toward that alley. I could identify him, if you need. Like I said, I saw the whole thing. No one else was around." By now he had caught his breath, but the adrenaline had kicked in and he wasn't gonna let nerves make it so this one got away. He sucked in air and waited for a response.

The cop remained eerily silent for a minute. The sounds of the city drowned everything else out as Alastair prayed that Diego wouldn't fuck this up by jumping in with some contradictory comment. He eyed him across the street and fortunately the man had the good sense to stay put.

Just when he thought that the Billy was going to shun him and speed away, he spoke for the first time, "What's there to show? If he took off when you said he did, he's not going to be anywhere near here. What's it to you, anyway?"

"That's the thing, I know who the guy is. He lives down that alley. I can show you where. He wouldn't have gone far."

The Billy said nothing, but nodded his head and dis-mounted the motorcycle. He towered over Alastair, had to be a good 6.2', built like an ox with his chest heaving in anticipation of violence. It was almost too much for Alastair. Even though they were all nearly identical, this one had that flair that made them all so appealing.

Alastair led him down the street toward the alley. They walked side by side, the cop refusing to walk behind him. They didn't exchange any words and Alastair wondered if the Billy was new to this, or was used to this kind of attention. He also wondered what had happened to Diego, but cared less with each step. Rounding the corner into the alley it became apparent that there were no houses or apartments down this way. A lone car sat parked behind the liquor store, probably that of the nervous clerk inside.

The Billy's steps slowed as the reality of the situation sank in. "Lives here in this alley you say..." his words trailed off, every one of them dripping with distrust.

"Yeah, well... I might not have actually seen him. But I saw you..." Alastair shifted from foot to foot waiting for the Billy's next move. He saw himself reflected in the cop's mirrored shades and wondered what he looked like in 056's eyes. Wondered what any of them see. If their view of the world was much different from anyone else's, or if they could actually be thought of as regular guys. He kept babbling, this one looked dubious, not like the last one at all even though he looked identical.

Abruptly, the cop cut him off, "Well, if he's not down here like you said," reaching down to his belt he unlatched the handcuffs, "we'll have to do something about it."

This is the moment. The one where things could go either way. The moment where the gamble either pays off, or if a night in a cell is at the other end of the conversation.

"Lean up against that car and put your hands behind your back."

The moment.

Alastair did as he was told, leaning forward with his sweating chest against the passenger door and bringing his hands around his back.

The Billy slapped on the cuffs.

"If you're thinking about..." Alastair's voice came out more shrill than intended.

"Shut up. On your knees. Turn around."

He did as ordered. Pants soaked up a grease stain from the asphalt. His heart pounded, not knowing if a blow to the head would come next, or another notch on his belt.

Silently Alastair waited for either fate, his face crotch level with the Billy. He eyed the gun, the taser, and the leather, then waited.

"Close your eyes."

Alastair waited for the death blow, but it didn't come.

"Open your mouth."

He obeyed. This is the moment he had hoped for, pined for, done crime for...

Before he could finish the thought the Billy was inside of him, all ten inches. He didn't wait to warm him up, but rather, plunged full on, finding the back of his throat immediately after entering. And he was rough, grabbing the back of Alastair's head and moving with it, bringing him up and down at the desired pace. Unrelenting in his motion. He aimed to cum, and cum fast.

Alastair gave in with complete abandon. Without fighting back he took the Billy in, moved with his hands, and tried to take him in even deeper. 056 growls at his near climax, pulled Alastair all the way in and unloaded in his mouth. He held it there for a minute, letting every drop find its way down his throat. Quivering he pulled out and zipped up.

"Get up. Turn around."

Alastair did as he was told. 056 removed the cuffs without a word and walked away down the alley back to his bike. Not a word. Just the way Alastair likes it. He wiped his lips and swallowed, waited a few minutes before following in the cop's direction, making sure not to be right on his heels. The Billy's boots echoed down the alley and then all went silent until Alastair heard the bike kick into action and speed away.

❊ 2 ❊

Arriving back at the station, 056 pulled his bike into the underground parking garage. After a long twelve-hour shift he was ready to get off of his feet, but before retiring for the night there would be mountains of paperwork to file for today's incidents. Identical bikes were parked in a line that extended most of the lot. Across from them a similar line of police cruisers awaited their nightly wash once the janitorial staff came in. The air was heavy with exhaust.

Slinging his jacket over his shoulder and pocketing his shades, 056 made his way up the stairs to the office, nodded at the receptionist, and made his way to the locker room to store his gear. The lockers were filled with Billys and other cops just ending their shifts. The "regular" cops kept to one side of the locker room, and the Billys to the other. The room was filled with the din of shop talk, everyone relaying the trials of their days.

056 spoke to no one, but gave several nods of acknowledgement as he moved toward his locker. One by one he pulled his knee-high boots off, followed by the rest of his uniform. The clothes he hung up to put in the queue for the dry cleaner, the boots he stored in the locker with the rest of his things. Now, fully nude, he made his way to the showers.

77

The shower room was filled with other Billys, all identical, and a smattering of other officers, again segregated to different sides of the room. Steam snaked its way through the air, fogging the windows and giving the showers their classic mystique. 056 found an empty shower head and started to rinse off the efforts of the day.

Crack! A wet towel hit him in the ass, eliciting a muffled cry and raising the skin to form a new welt next to the others. The guys had really been riding him lately, and this time he'd barely had the opportunity to get wet before they laid into him.

"Very funny, guys. You wanna try that while I'm looking?"

No one responded but several other snaps lit up the room as the guys fooled around with each other, trading blows with their wet towels. The Billys and other cops, as usual, weren't mixing, but each side of the room traded playful blows, slaps on the ass, and a variety of shit talk echoed through the showers.

"Hey donkey dicks, pick up any tricks today?" The shout came from the "regular" cop side of the room.

No one responded. For a second the showers fell quiet and all you could hear was the running of the water. Seconds ticked by like minutes and a few of the wet towels hit the floor. Several men left.

"Yeah, they've got nothing to say, as usual. Donkey dick fuckers. Hell, they're not even real men. Are you guys? Bunch of pretty boys."

Another of the regular cops joined in the banter, "Judging by their records they're probably more man than you are, Daniels. Feeling a little self-conscious, are you?"

Daniels scoffed loudly. It was true that several of the guys had lost jobs to the Billys, and no new hires had come in for a while. But they did do a damn good job.

The perfect model of a cop, each and every one of them. And pretty. Too pretty.

056 started rinsing the soap off and eyed Daniels. The man was stout, built thick, and had a receding hairline. Not a bad looking guy, but not a perfect specimen. And he obviously knew it. None of the guys really were, but they didn't have to be. It wasn't part of the job. The Billys, however, were all chiseled. Identical, and all in the same room, they came off as an intimidating force. And perhaps that was the point. Yet, it just happened quite by happenstance that the original that they were modeled from, more so for his track record than his looks, happened to also be tall, handsome, and well hung. His attractiveness was missed on some of the guys, them being more interested in women. But the Billys were used to turning heads. And being resented for it.

Daniels wasn't pleased. "Records my ass. They built these fuckers to steal our jobs. They'll be phasing you out along with the rest of us. Just wait and see."

A cold silence spread through the showers. He'd said what everyone had been thinking, but none dared to voice. Change was coming. And when it happened quickly, no one liked it.

✻   3   ✻

"Hey! You can't go back there. Employees only. Get the hell out!" The store clerk was as angry as he was afraid. Dealing with this kind of shit was above his pay grade. And it happened all too often. "Out! Or I'll call the cops."

That was what Diego had been waiting for. He pocketed a pack of smokes and leapt over the counter to flee out the door. But not in too much of a hurry. The clerk wouldn't do anything. Even if he was armed, he wouldn't get into anything that serious, or dangerous, over petty theft. Let it be the boss's problem.

Diego casually strode down the aisle toward the back door, as if he owned the place. Entering the alley, he had to shield his eyes from the direct sunlight, giving them a moment to adjust to being outside. The clerk was probably calling the cops right now. But would they show up for only a pack of smokes? *I should have emptied the cash register before getting out of there.* But it was too late for that now. Going back in as an afterthought wasn't a good idea.

He took a seat on the curb and unwrapped the package to light one up. Sitting in the shade felt good, and so did a fresh smoke. Having been on the bum for the past few weeks had left him jonesing for the small comforts, and the big ones. He almost couldn't remember the last time he'd gotten laid. He waited for the sirens. *Where are they already?* That familiar sound wasn't coming. Against his better judgement he walked around the block back to the front of the store.

The clerk was standing out front talking to a man wearing a regular suit. He didn't look like a cop, but he did have that authoritarian voice, as if the victim was also the perpetrator of some grievous crime. *Plain clothes?* Diego walked closer.

"That's him. That's the guy. Fucking idiot came back." The clerk's voice was frantic as he pointed wildly in Diego's direction. The man in the suit followed the finger and his eyes landed square on Diego.

Oh shit. It's not a Billy. But it is the fuzz. He had fucked up. And it was time to go.

Diego took off running back to the alley he had just left, beating pavement as though his life depended on it. His footsteps were echoed by another pair of feet. The cop had taken off after him. Not the usual plain clothes reaction. But he was coming, closing the distance between them quickly.

Diego's lungs felt like they had caught fire. He was still holding the cigarette as he ran; realizing this, he tossed it aside. Exercise wasn't what he had signed up for. His breathing became shallow as he grew increasingly winded. The alley stretched out before him in a straight shot. There was nowhere to duck into, he'd have to outrun the cop. Which was feeling progressively less likely.

The shout came from behind him.

"You might as well give it up. Evading arrest isn't really worth a few lousy smokes."

The cop had a point. But giving up wasn't in the plan. If they took him down to the station, there would be Billys there. Not exactly a private place, though. *What was I thinking going back there?* He ran on, hoping that the cop was getting as tired as he was, that both of their legs were protesting the impromptu flight.

But the echoing sound of boots hitting the pavement was getting closer and he knew that he was had. He gave it one last go. Mustered up the last of his strength and tried to sprint. His ankle twisted and before he even hit the ground the cop was on top of him, cuffs out and on his wrists before he could even try to protest.

"Thought you could get away, did you? Now you're mine." He put his knee deeper into Diego's back.

"Nice try. You're no Billy."

The plain clothes scoffed and flipped Diego over. He stared him in the eyes with a strange mix of contempt and desire.

"So, you're one of the Billy Club are you? We've heard of you perverts. Well, those fake prefab cops ain't the real thing. And you're gonna find out." He moved to unclasp his belt.

For a moment Diego squirmed, trying to get out from under him. *But it's been so long.* His mind changed just like that. He stopped fighting and gave in. And for all he knew the cop was right. He'd been after Billys so long he almost couldn't remember what it felt like to have another face panting above him.

"Get up. Move. Over there." He pointed to a nearby tree, a giant magnolia with a monstrous trunk.

Diego did as he was told and slowly moved to the back side of the tree. The cop led him from behind by the cuffs and pressed him up against the bark. He yanked Diego's pants down with one hand while holding the cuffs by the chain with the other. Pulling down the zipper on his pants, he pulled his cock out.

"You gonna do this or not?" Diego taunted him. He knew this kind of guy. The kind who liked control as much as he did sex, probably even more so. "Get on with it."

The cop responded by spitting in his hand and rubbing it on his stiffening cock. Without warning he lifted Diego's cuffed hands causing a little bit of deliberate pain, and, still standing, slid his member straight into Diego's ass.

Letting out a small grunt Diego took him in. "You gonna read me my rights?" Now he was goading him.

"Remain silent. That's all you're gonna get."

Diego did as he was told. Words had no place between them anymore. Just flesh.

Eltrop servingled oppringing on his hand and got
binger on his stuttering cook. Without woming he licked
Diego pulled hands someons a little blood realise...
pump unducing Tanmiese, slit his newsber designation
Diego isn...

Letting her a small group Diego come maynen... You
gonna read me mare here?"... now Tanik is counting blue
Kenmal steat, There all sable pourt.
Deeg did say, you cook, Woof War had more be
neven then sarvior, just flesh.

✸   4   ✸

"You seen Diego around lately?" Jacky asked.

Alastair shrugged off the question. He hadn't. Not for days. And when he had the guy had been next to useless, as usual. He lit a smoke and said nothing.

"Used to see you guys around together all the time. Something go down? Thought you two were an item."

He couldn't help but laugh. An item! Hell, they were barely friends. Hung around the same blocks, that's all. "Naw. Nothing between us. He probably got pinched, knowing that guy. I've got more important things to worry about."

Alastair leaned up against the bus stop ad and blew out a cloud of smoke which mingled with the exhaust coming from the thick line of cars. A light drizzle started to fall on the city streets, releasing the smell of asphalt.

"We really gonna stand around here right in front of this hot car? Red handed, if you ask me." Jacky was shifting from foot to foot, growing increasingly nervous the longer they hung around.

Alastair shot him a serious look. "Would kinda defeat the purpose if we took off. Shut up and wait."

Across the street from them the stolen car sat

parked conspicuously. They had left the windows down and several street dwellers passing by had already reached in the windows, rifling around the console for change or smokes, leaving empty handed and sauntering off into the rain.

They'd been standing there for almost an hour with no sign of the cops, and not a single Billy. But it was only a matter of time. A nice car like that wouldn't usually be seen in a neighborhood like this, definitely not with the windows down. Everything about the car screamed: stolen.

Alastair ground the cigarette butt out underfoot and lit another.

"How many of those are you gonna smoke before you realize that this is a fool's errand?" Jacky sat down on the bus stop bench and quickly stood back up again.

Without looking in his direction Alastair said, "It's like waiting for the bus. You light one up and it arrives. Works with Billys too." But the superstition hadn't paid off so far.

But this time it did. A patrol car pulled around the corner and slowly cruised up the boulevard toward them. When it sighted the out of place car it slowed further and pulled up next to it. A beam of light shone out of the spotlight mounted in the window and penetrated the interior of the car, then moved down toward the license plate.

The beam halted there as the patrol car idled, presumably running the plates.

"Now?" asked Jacky.

Alastair shushed him, "Quiet. Just wait and see. I'll show you how it's done." He had no way of knowing the badge number in the darkened cab of the car, but he could tell by the silhouette that they had lured a Billy. Most cops didn't have that ideal profile.

As he stepped out of the patrol car it was obvious that his face wasn't the only perfect thing about him. A

Billy all right. His long legs, with leather boots up to the knees, led up to that big bold chest. But the badge number was still obscured by the darkness. Alastair almost pulled out his small binoculars, but this close the cop might see him do it and get suspicious. He decided against it. He'd have to go in cold.

Dodging oncoming cars, he leap-frogged across the street advancing on the lone cop. The Billy was continuing his loop around the car, shining his mag-light through all the windows, checking for god-knew-what. In cop fashion everything could be suspicious. Drugs, a sleeping homeless man, a body... He was proceeding cautiously, just like they all did... Until something more fun came up.

Alastair made it across the street and approached him.

"Jaywalking is illegal. You're lucky that I'm in the middle of something." said the Billy, without looking up at him.

Alastair leaned up against the deep red finish of the car. "I hope you're right."

"What?"

"That I'm lucky. That's what I was hoping for."

For a second the Billy looked confused. Then he shined the light into Alastair's face. Recognition spread across his handsome mug. "Oh, it's you. You have a strange habit of hanging around crime scenes."

"Oh, is this a crime scene? How exciting." His voice higher than usual, Alastair did his best to look innocent and toed the ground like a schoolgirl.

The cop lowered his flashlight, running the beam down Alastair's body. With the light out of his eyes he could finally see the badge number.

Damn. The number registered in his mind. 015. He already had a notch for this one. Finding new Billys was getting harder and harder. Even though he had been rotating neighborhoods. Maybe the cops did the same thing. Some folks found the Billys disconcerting. Seeing the same face over and over again could be eerie. But not for Alastair. *Fuck it. There's nothing else to do.* And having risked a car theft there was no way he was going to back out of this one with no reward.

Alastair leaned back up against the car and smoothed his jacket, rain plashing off and into the gutter.

"You remember me?"

The Billy looked annoyed. "You street rats all look the same. How should I know?"

"We all look the same? That's a good one."

The cop didn't look pleased with the quip. His hand found its way down to his gun belt and fondled the latch.

Alastair followed his hand and grew increasingly nervous. He thought about stealing a look back at Jacky but didn't want to take his eyes off the firearm. He had probably run off by now anyway.

"Are you serious? You know me."

"Yeah, I know all about you. And your kind. Now get in the car." He gestured toward the hot red ride, not the patrol car.

A lump formed in Alastair's throat. He swallowed hard in anticipation. If he got in the car, he would be a suspect for the theft, and there was no way around it. Of course, he had stolen the car, but so far there was nothing to connect him with the crime. The Billy didn't care.

What's this guy up to? Does he even remember me? But Alastair stopped questioning and got in the backseat as indicated.

The Billy looked around for a second. The traffic had thinned while the downpour had thickened. No pedestrians were in sight. The cop climbed in the back-seat and on top of Alastair. The cuffs were out and on one of Alastair's wrists before he could even feign protest. The other snapped down on the handle of the door, pinning Alastair to the bucket seat.

Last time, when he had encountered 015, it had been in the back room of a bar. The place had been full of people but the back room had been empty except for them. It had been slow, they were in no hurry, and Alastair couldn't even remember how he had drawn the Billy out to the club.

Now, in the back of a stolen car, everything moved quickly. His pants were around his ankles before he knew it. The Billy was inside of him seconds later. And the car windows steamed up, blocking out the rainy street beyond.

Alastair hadn't even had time to entice the man, barely had begun the flirting, had almost missed the badge number. So, the Billy definitely remembered him, or the Billy Club was bigger than Alastair imagined. And there'd be no new conquest tonight. His number would remain the same. Jacky hadn't even stayed around to watch. And he was distracted by being in the back of the hot car.

With a grunt the Billy shot inside of him, let his body down loose on top of him and then wetly pulled out, all before Alastair could respond. 015 backed out of the vehicle, zipped up his fly, and fastened his belt.

Alastair didn't mind an abrupt exit. But with the cuffs still on, he wasn't going anywhere. He held up his wrist as best he could, jangling the cuff to get the Billy's attention, but 015 just said something into his radio and ignored Alastair.

"Hey man, what the fuck? You gonna let me out of here?"

015 said nothing and walked back to the patrol car, got in, and revved up the engine. Alastair started to yell something, but it was covered up by the whoop whoop of the siren as the Billy pulled into oncoming traffic and took off.

❅ 5 ❅

Jacky had watched for a few moments before realizing that their "team" effort wasn't going to get him anywhere. *Fucking selfish prick.* He walked off slowly, rain drenching his coat, and wishing that he had brought an umbrella. A distant siren started getting closer. Catching a bus out of there would have been preferable, but waiting at the bus stop wasn't an option. He pulled out a smoke but a fat raindrop promptly soiled it.

Waiting around for Alastair wasn't going to happen. Not while he was having all the fun and there was no reward for Jacky's part in the grand theft auto. *What a waste!* It would have been better just to keep the car, at least for a while. Still, after all he had heard about the Billys, he was wanting a taste and wanting it bad.

He plodded on through the wet, empty street. There was nothing for blocks and he was already soaked. *Alastair is so full of shit. He just uses everyone to get what he wants.* But he had known that already and had gone along with the ride in futile hopes of something more. Then again, the night was still young and there had to be some boys still lurking around the streets somewhere.

The rain continued to get worse, and trash was now

being pushed along with the deluge, clogging up the street drains and causing it to flood onto the sidewalks. His boots were soaked. Up ahead the red neon of a bar beckoned. At least it would be dry inside. Maybe someone would take pity on his soaked clothes and buy him a beer, or he could lollygag one at the very least.

As empty as the street was, the bar was full. TVs blared from every wall, each playing an identical hockey game. Cheers and shouts came from the crowd as a goal was scored and rival fans gave each other friendly shit. Several of the guys standing at the bar were in uniform, drinking after their long shifts. Jacky cleared the water from his eyes, took off his soiled hat, and stared down the line of them. Billys. He'd walked straight into a cop haunt. But from the identical faces he knew it wasn't a regular cop bar. The Billys had claimed a place of their own.

He moved up to the polished oak and tried to look nonchalant as he put his foot up on the bar. The barkeep was busy watching the game and paid him no mind as another goal was scored and the crowd lit up with hoots and hollers. While the Billy next to him was occupied with the screen he reached out and snagged his almost full pint, and started sipping on it like it had been his all along.

For the next few minutes the game heated up and kept the off duty cops busy with their fan squabbles and rabblerousing. The Billy next to him reached out for his beer, hand swiping through the air, finding only the empty spot where he had last set it down. He swiped again, and this time, when finding nothing, he looked over at Jacky with an expressionless face.

The Billy mouthed the words, "What the fuck..."

Jacky attempted to look like he fit in. Sad, wet puppy dog eyes gazing around the room, looking for a place to shrink to, only found a room full of heat. It was the lion's den, a full room of Billys, and he was on his own. Alastair would have lost his shit, but he wasn't around, nor would he be.

"Hey you!" the Billy shouted over the din.

In that moment Jacky caught a glimpse of his badge, number 087. His eyes moved up from his chest to his face, meeting eyes for the first time.

"Where do you get off snaking my beer? You've got some nerve."

Jacky's mouth moved up and down silently looking for an excuse. The cop's mouth altered into a wicked smile.

"You could have just asked, if you're hard up. But it's too late for that now." his smile drooped into stern blankness.

"Wait. I can repay you. It's just that..."

Before he could finish his proposal, the Billy had swept his legs out from under him, splashing the stolen beer all over his face while he hit the ground. The Billy, and those around him who had seen, all started to laugh.

"Repay me, you say. And how you gonna do that?"

The laughter continued, until it stopped. And then the bar was silent aside from the TVs, and the whole room was looking down at him on the floor, waiting for his next move.

Jacky slowly got himself up, holding onto the bar until he was upright and face to face with the cop that had put him on his ass.

Attempting to regain his composure he repeated, "I can repay you. Buy me another beer and I'll give you something even more worthwhile."

At this 087 straightened up and towered over Jacky. His blank expression became a smirk.

"All right. You've got balls. I like that. Tender, get this guy a beer and let's see what he's got up his sleeve." The boys lining the bar all started to laugh again before most of them turned their attention back to the game.

When the beer arrived, Jacky slammed it down in one gulp, unsure of what he was getting himself into. He eyed 087 and saw that two other Billys sitting next to him were also glaring his way, hungry looks in their eyes.

087 stood up. "Ok, you've had enough. Time for payback." He took Jacky by the shoulder and pushed him past the bar toward the back room. The Billys next to him got up as well and trailed a few steps behind. No one else took mind, but, as they passed, Jacky could see the barkeep snickering as he wiped a glass clean.

Like a death row inmate on his way to the gallows, Jacky paced through the bar with the Billy's hand still on his shoulder until he reached an unmarked door in the back of the room. The Billy pushed him inside and the others followed.

The door swung shut and Jacky could hear the door latch as the last in the line locked them in. None of them said anything as 087 threw him down onto the lone table that sat in the center of the room. The other two came onto him, aggressively yanked his wet pants off, and flipped him over.

087 came up behind him and shoved his cock in his ass without warning. Before Jacky could cry out his mouth was filled with dick. The third Billy stood to the side and removed his piece as well, stroking it with his hand and staring at Jacky's bare ass. 087 raised the wet shirt exposing his lower back. Seconds later hot cum splashed Jacky's skin and filled his mouth at the same time. The third Billy took 087's place and crammed his identical dick into his gaping hole. 087 moved to the front and stuck his still quivering cock into Jacky's mouth, pouring the last drops of cum into him, mingling with the full load. The cop that he'd sucked off unlocked the door and left without a word as the other two continued to have their way with him.

087's dick went limp and then hard again as he

started to work Jacky's mouth with greater force. The pounding on his ass intensified and like a pig on a spit he was yanked back and forth with the cops' alternating motions, until they started banging away in synched rhythm. He couldn't breathe, but then the cop behind him slowed down, and with one last thrust emptied into him. This was followed with another blast into his mouth as 087 came again.

087 left the room without a word as the other cop zipped his fly back up.

"Now get the fuck out of here before we beat your ass and haul you in. And make it quick." he left without anything further to say, leaving Jacky panting on the table.

❦   6   ❦

Still cuffed in the car, Alastair heard a vehicle skid to a halt followed by the beam of a flashlight hitting his sweat covered face. He was a sitting duck.

Laughter surrounded the car. "Well, well, look at what we've got here."

"Got ourselves a stuck little pig, do we" a second voice sounded.

The flashlight beams crossed each other, scanning the rest of the car to see if anything else was inside. Satisfied that there wasn't, two of the car doors opened in unison. The one he was cuffed to yanked his arm, forcing out a grunt of pain.

Alastair had managed to get his pants back up before they had arrived, but he could feel cum slowly dripping out of him. His wrist was sore from the too-tight cuffs. So was his back from laying in such an awkward prone position. He couldn't see the men, but their laughter was ominous. The night wasn't going to be all fun and games.

"Hey Daniels, should we let him simmer a while? Probably the only time in his life that scum like this gets to enjoy such a nice ride." The speaker was tapping his night stick against the side of the vehicle.

"Go ahead if you want to, but my shift is gonna end soon. I've got better things to do than fool around out here in the slums," he said, as he circled around the car to his partner's side.

They spoke in hushed tones to each other for a while. Alastair couldn't make out the words, but their cadence was decidedly cop. Neither of them a Billy. There was no point in struggling, they were going to do whatever they wanted with him.

The door moved again, and he thought it would rip his arm out of the socket. He stifled a cry. He heard the jingling sound of keys accompanied by another wrench of his arm, and then it was free. He instinctively brought it up to cover his face and crunched his body into fetal position.

"Fun's over. Get up and get out, you piece of shit!" It was Daniels' voice. His partner was still laughing.

For a moment Alastair remained frozen before he realized that if a beating was coming, he would be taking it on his feet rather than lying in the back of the car. He slowly brought his knees around and scooched out the passenger side backdoor to where the cops were waiting. Before he was fully erect, handcuffs were being slapped on his wrists again. They bit into the already sore flesh.

They handled him roughly and in a hurry. Shoving him into the back of their patrol car, his head hit against the doorframe on the way in, adding injury to insult. They threw him the rest of the way in, slammed the door, and entered their respective sides, leaving him sprawled out in the backseat, hands cuffed behind his back and struggling to right his position. The car peeled out into the street and sped off.

When they had got the speed up Daniels slammed on the brakes, throwing Alastair against the divider separating the front from the back. They burst out in peals of laughter as they did this over and over, humiliating and hurting Alastair more with each slam of the brakes. Just cops having fun and there was nothing he could do about it. They kept it up most of the way to the station. Finally it stopped as they pulled into the parking garage.

They removed him as gingerly as they had put him in, yanking him to his feet and pushing him forward toward the entrance to the station.

"What charge are you booking me on? I didn't steal anything."

A slap to the back of the head. "Shut up and move." Another shove to the small of the back.

"Hey Daniels. You're getting off now. Go ahead and get out of here. I'll finish booking this trash. It's been a long enough day already. I'll see you at the bar later. Keep one cold for me."

"Thanks, man. Roger that. Catch you later."

And he was off. Alastair could hear Daniels' boots pound off down the hallway, the other cop's words blurring into meaninglessness as he was signed in with the all too familiar procedure. He zoned out for the rest of the process until he heard the bars of his new cell slam shut behind him.

"So they got you too?"

Alastair turned around to see Diego standing at the cell wall next to several other men. The others were silent, remaining several feet away from Diego, as if in distaste for the man. None of them had that fresh look of discomfort on their faces, suggesting that all had been occupying the cells for at least a few days.

"Oh, it's you. How long have you been in?" Alastair said flatly.

Diego looked around the room, as if to see whether anyone was watching him. "It's been two days, maybe three. Haven't seen much of the guards, except when they bring in someone new. There's been no word about further processing."

For a while they were all silent. The whir of a ceiling vent and buzz of the fluorescents was the only sound. Even the rain was blocked out by the thick plexiglass window, too high up and too small to let in any real light or sound. The room had the tang of unwashed bodies.

Finally, Alastair broke the silence, "Any of the guards Billys?"

"Not that I've seen. Not many guards have come by at all, but the ones that did were all normies. I think that..."

"Yeah, yeah. The Billys are all beats. Just hoping that they might pay a visit anyway." Several of the other men snickered at this. The other two turned away toward the wall in disgust. Their problem, if they didn't know the pleasures of the Billys.

A loud clang rang through the room followed by the rusty creak of trolley wheels. The guard struck his club against the bars again, bringing the men to attention.

"You shut up in there. Quiet, and up against the wall. Slop time."

They had no choice but to obey. If one of them fucked this up it would mean no food until tomorrow. And the guard looked like he was itching to use his baton. They did as they were told and the guard slowly unloaded the trolley, putting each of the trays on the floor by the door of the cell.

When the door slammed back shut, one of the men against the wall said, "Hey. How long are they holding us here? Isn't this supposed to be temporary? Aren't they moving us soon?"

The guard said nothing and moved on. The food suggested that no one was going anywhere tonight.

"Fuck it. Might as well make the most of it." Alastair retrieved his tray and sat down cross-legged to eat.

The others followed suit, and the whir of the fan was drowned out by the sounds of eating.

With his mouth full Diego asked, "Any new notches since I saw you last?"

"Shut the fuck up. What do you care? Although, without you around, it's easier to attract just about anything."

Diego looked hurt but kept shoveling the slop into his mouth. The men had all separated to different sides of the cell to eat. Not far enough away from each other to make much of a difference, but a silent form of protest to express their distaste for the Billy Club guys. One man had remained next to Diego and Alastair, and he spoke up.

"How many?"

"What's it to you?" sneered Alastair.

"Forty-eight."

Diego turned his head and stopped chewing. "What?"

"I said forty-eight."

Now Alastair chimed in, "Forty-eight what?"

The man stood up and looked down on them. "Billys, you idiots. Forty-eight Billys. How many notches you got?"

Both men gasped. His numbers were way higher than theirs. And neither of them knew if the Billy badge numbers were linear, sporadic, or if there was a rhyme or reason to the numbers at all. Each kept a mental list as if keeping score on a score card, but neither had really thought about just how many of them there were. Forty-eight put the Billys into a different context altogether.

Diego said, "So, you're part of the ever so informal Billy Club. Have they caught on yet? Sounds like you've known a few."

The man said, "Oh yeah, they know. So do the normies. Those fuckers think it's funny. Also heard rumors that the regular cops want to use it to discredit the program. They're all hot under the collar about it.

Heard a few arguing about how it all makes the department look bad. But crime is apparently down since they were introduced, so they're having a time of it."

Alastair said, "Damn. Forty-eight. I thought I was good. You know how many of them there are? Diego here isn't anywhere near you, I'm getting close though."

Diego rolled his eyes at the jab. So far, he had only been with twelve. Alastair had kept his number private, but, considering all the ones Diego had been around for, his number must be high. But obviously not up to forty-eight yet.

The man said, "A friend of mine says he's been with nearly seventy. We've been keeping track of badge numbers. Figure they're linear. Highest one either of us has seen is 100. That's been my goal, all hundred. But my pal, he has other ideas."

One hundred made sense. The cops liked things nice and even. A good round number. The first wave of an experiment in the new police state. Maybe they had unleashed a hundred Billys into every city. Maybe they would have to travel around and find out once they were done with this batch. They were so good that they would probably be replacing the normies, if some scandal didn't take down the program first. That had an appeal in and of itself; fuck the system till it breaks.

Diego started to speak but Alastair shushed him.

"What other ideas?" Alastair's tone was nothing but serious.

The man paced around for a minute, took in the disdainful looks of the guys across the room, and continued, "My guess is that like me, you've been shooting to nail them all. Looks like I've come a little closer than you have. Anyway, all in a day's work. But my pal, he's got a theory," He stopped his pacing for a moment, looked at them in the face for effect, and started moving around the room again, this time speaking in a hushed tone, "See, they clone the perfect cop, right?

Clean up the streets and what not. But he's got this one weakness that no one wants to talk about except for the normies. But think about it...where did they get, I mean, how would they build such a perfect specimen? There's got to be an original. We think he's out there somewhere. That's our Golden Goose. Sure, the Billys are hot. And you're damn right I'm gonna hit them all. But the original...the others are just copies. We aim to find him."

Alastair and Diego looked at each other in stunned silence. Why hadn't it occurred to them? They had been so busy chasing Billys that they had never stopped to think about how they had come to be. Golden Goose indeed.

From the other side of the room, "Shut the fuck up you perverts. I don't want to hear about your creepy shit." The others sitting next to the speaker concurred with grunts of approval.

"What's it to you? Mind your own fucking business!" Diego had found a use for himself, finally.

The guy that had spoken stood up, towering a good six inches over Diego. "You gonna make me?" Slowly he advanced on the three, fists balled, anger in his eyes. Alastair stepped between them attempting to cool things down.

"Hey, hey, buddy. We're just having a private conversation over here. Nothing to concern yourself over."

The man didn't find his words amusing at all. Hate flashed in his eyes. It was *that* look.

Without waiting or warning Alastair dropped to one knee and socked the guy in the stomach. He doubled over and Alastair shot his left straight up into the chin that was falling toward him. The man's body arced in the other direction now, sending him in a graceful curve backwards. He hit the floor like wet pasta.

Diego and their friendly cellmate picked up the limp body and threw him back in the corner with the others, the ones who had grunted approval were now silent. Diego glowered at them, but they kept looking at the floor.

"Now that that's sorted out...I'd love to see what you've got that's so good almost fifty Billys can't resist. Is it how you draw them in or how you make them stay? How about giving me a piece of that."

"You're on your own, pal. I'm gonna be the first to have all hundred. And the original. And I'm saving it for them. You two suck each other off and figure it out yourselves. But then again, you're too stupid to have realized what's going on in the first place. Maybe you should just skip to another town and see if the Billys are easier in suburbia."

Alastair's fist still ached but he was about ready to use it again. Diego sensed the violence and stepped in closer. All three tensed and stood taller. A bead of sweat rolled down Alastair's forehead and past his eye, mimicking the path of a tear. The guys in the corner stirred in anticipation next to the still knocked out loudmouth.

Alastair broke the heated silence, "So do I have to hit you or are you gonna let me hit that?"

All three broke out in laughter. The men in the corner turned away.

Still laughing he dropped trou and leaned up against the wall. Alastair spit in his hands and rubbed it on his cock, saving some and rubbing it between the man's cheeks. He used his foot to kick out the man's leg, spreading his stance further. Diego licked his lips as he watched and pulled out his piece, stroking it between thumb and forefingers.

Alastair entered him with ease. The Billys had primed the man and Alastair's cock slid right in without resistance. Face against the wall he grunted with pleasure as Alastair worked his way deeper. As he quickened his pace, he moved his gaze to the men in the corner who were still shying away.

"Don't you want to watch fellas?" Taunting them made his dick harder still.

He took his time, moving in and out while Diego moved with his hand and stepped closer in offering his dick to the guy up against the wall. Between pants he reached out and cupped the member in his hand, jerking it to the same rhythm of Alastair's pumping.

Diego shot his load onto the man's wrist with his head back in pleasure grimace pleasure, grimacing. The man brought his hand to his mouth and licked off the cum that hadn't made its way to the floor. Alastair moved quicker and deeper, slamming his body into the man's back side with increasing fervor. The moans got louder, and, with a final sustained grunt, Alastair filled the man's ass with hot cum.

"You want a turn on this, Diego?" He backed up letting his cock fall out followed by hot drips of cum.

Diego didn't waste any time and, stroking his cock hard again, replaced Alastair behind the guy, entering him quickly and getting into the motion. Their cellmate, still up against the wall, took him in without resistance and moaned deeply with each thrust. Alastair watched on with terrible pleasure.

Cum mixed with cum as Diego burst again, less jizz this time, but with more gusto than a hand job could accomplish. He kneeled down and licked the cum now leaking out of the man's further loosened ass, trying to get every last drop. When he felt that he had gotten it all, he stood back up and leaned in to kiss the man, transferring the cooling loads into his mouth.

Alastair, head leaned back, laughed in pure pleasure, his dick starting to rise again.

The familiar sound of a night stick rattling against the bars down the hall broke through the bacchanal, and all the men in the cell stood at attention in the back of the room away from the door. None dared speak in the presence of a guard.

❧ 7 ❧

Jacky stood on the corner across from the bar watching Billys come and go out the front door. There was probably more action out back, but he kept thinking that his friends might show. Word could have spread about the Billy Bar after he had told his story to a few of the guys on the street. He pulled out a bottle of rush and took a deep inhale. His head lit up, and he flushed.

There'd been no sign of Alastair, or that idiot Diego, for days. But oh, would they come flocking once they heard about this place. For now, it was all Jacky's. This time he had come with a few bucks in his pocket. No use starting things out wrong, he wanted his pick this time. Didn't want to risk getting thrown out, either. He wanted to take his time.

The front door opened, and he saw a slice of light puncture the red glowing darkness out front. Inside, from what he could see, looked packed. Identical faces smiling, tipping back pints, and general carousal. Music thumped out into the street.

The door shut again, muting the music, and making Jacky impatient. Rumors usually spread quicker on the street, and he figured he wouldn't be going at it alone tonight. They probably hadn't caught word, or they would have showed by now. Alastair, at least, wouldn't miss this for the world. He hit the rush again and started to cross.

As he stepped off the curb, white vans came skidding around the corner, slamming on the brakes in front of the bar. Another van kept going and circled to the back. It looked like a raid but, with nothing but cops inside, that seemed doubtful. Jacky took a step back and into the shadows, waiting to see what was happening.

Men stormed out of the vans, some in plain clothes, others in uniform. They were cops, but from the looks of them they weren't here to drink. Their movement suggested they had already been into the bottle. Jacky saw some of their faces when the door opened, letting out the light. They weren't Billys, it was the regular cops, and they didn't look happy.

What the fuck!? Jacky took a few more steps backwards and bumped into a wrought iron fence; he crouched to blend in with the bushes behind the fence. It was probably safer to get the hell out of there, but he wanted to see where this was going. He'd never seen so many off duty cops at once, all in one place.

The brawl spilled out into the street from both sides of the building. A storm of fists were raining down throughout the throng. A chaos of shouting and cries disturbed the night. Cops were everywhere from the curb to the middle of the street and filling the parking lot behind the bar. Jacky saw several guys go down followed by a flurry of legs kicking and the flash of several night sticks.

The fight was vicious and cruel. Jacky had never seen anything like it, but he knew he had clearly picked a bad night to go cruising at the bar. He kept his distance, watching in fascination. If only the other guys were here to see this. He pulled out his phone and started snapping pictures before switching it to video and capturing as much of the fight as he could in the low light.

$\mathscr{X}$ 8 $\mathscr{X}$

Alastair stood on the steps outside of the jail, going over the stuff in his pockets to make sure it was all there. He found his pack of smokes intact and lit one up, relishing the smoke after two days of enforced quitting. He eyed the street both ways, considering what to do next now that he was out.

As he was deciding, he heard someone call out his name from the front door. For a second, he thought of bolting, that they had made some kind of mistake in letting him out and were now reconsidering. Out of breath, Diego ran up to him from behind.

"So, they let you out, too?" Diego was still panting, high on the new freedom.

Alastair handed him a smoke. "Looks like we're both free men now. They didn't really have anything to hold me on. Being found in a stolen car isn't exactly the same as being caught stealing one."

Diego shook his head, taking in the irony. "Yeah, all they had me for was a pack of smokes," he exhaled a large cloud after holding it in, relishing it for a second too long and coughing, "Let me out on time served."

"Let's get the fuck outta here. I need a drink."

Diego concurred. Anywhere but the jailhouse was preferable. They took off down the dirty street away from the station. On the end of the block, they bought a nickel bag from some guys loitering around the parking garage. Dealing right under the noses of the cops, where they wouldn't bother to pay attention.

Passing the joint back and forth they headed east, each step shaking off the forced confinement. Not three blocks from the station Jacky came running up to them, panting and babbling too fast to be coherent.

Alastair put his hand on Jacky's shoulder. "Slow down, man. Whatever it is I'm sure it can wait a second. We're basking in our newfound freedom; don't harsh our mellow." He handed the joint to Jacky to slow his roll. "There's a watering hole just up the block. Let's get a drink and you can tell us all about it, in private.

The three of them made their way into the bar and found a dark booth in the corner, one facing the door, so that they could see whoever came in after them. Jacky told them all about what he had seen and showed them the footage and pictures.

Above Alastair's laughter Diego said, "That's fucking crazy, man. No one saw you there, are you sure?"

"You saw the video, those guys were too busy kicking each other's asses to notice one guy across the street. I never seen anything like it."

Alastair's laughter had ceased. He put a hand on each of their shoulders, one on each side. "You guys have any idea what we've got here? I'm sure they tidied it up quietly, but do you have any idea what a scandal this would cause for the department? Gives me a bigger idea."

He had both of their attention. And he paused for effect.

"Jacky, a Billy bar! You're a genius for finding this place, and I hope you laid as many of them as you could before this shit started. So, that's brilliant. But this video, man. This shit could really stir things up. And we can make it worse. With Jacky's video skills and this cock," he grabbed his crotch, "we could make a whole other video that would fuck up the department for good. Catch my drift?"

Recognition spread across Diego's and Jacky's faces.

"It's broad daylight. Are you sure this is the way to do it?" Diego paced nervously as Alastair peered around the corner at the bar and Jacky stayed hidden across the street with his camera at the ready. "It's not like they're gonna meet up for a drink before their shift." Diego's voice was wary from lack of sleep.

"How do you know that? You been hanging around this place? You got some inside insight on these guys that I don't?" Alastair liked being questioned by Diego almost as much as he liked being up this early. "Besides, we gotta do this in broad daylight. For the cameras. But also for the impression. I can see the headlines now."

Across the street Jacky gave them the thumbs up, but the street remained deserted, even though the bar had been open for an hour or so. They hadn't seen a single Billy enter or leave, or anyone for that matter.

Still pacing Diego couldn't help but break the silence, "Maybe we should try the donut shop or something. Those guys are probably getting coffee on their way to the station. If this takes any longer, I'm gonna go in and get a drink. Anything is better than standing around in the cold. You gotta be tired by now, too."

"Don't you see the point? Sure, we could find a Billy at the donut shop. But what news would that be? And do you find that hot? Naw, we gotta catch one in the act of fucking up. Stain the reputation. The dumpster behind the bar, that's our setting. The film is gonna be a masterpiece. Wouldn't you wanna watch it?"

Diego could see that he had a point. "But if there's no Billy, there's no film."

"Always impatient. They always come. Even if I gotta cause a stir, they'll be here. Just you wait. But when he does come, you stay out of it. Can't have you fucking this up and them catching onto to us. Jacky was lucky to catch the brawl, we ain't gonna keep getting lucky for long if you botch this."

Bored and belittled, Diego lit a smoke and sat down on the curb. This passive role bullshit was getting old. The wait didn't seem to bother Jacky or Alastair, but this shit was boring, all this waiting around for something to happen. Hadn't they come for action?

Jacky started waving at them from his hiding place across the street. A patrol car pulled into the parking lot. The black and white pulled snug into an open spot and a Billy got out of the car, one long leg at a time. Without even looking around, he entered the bar.

CHAPTER THIRTY-SIX

❧ 10 ❧

Jacky pushed record and watched the small screen come into focus. The Billy came out of the bar, walking confidently. He'd only been in there long enough for one drink, maybe two. But that was enough to get the point across. The lens zoomed in as Alastair came trotting across the street toward the patrol car.

"Hey, hey, officer." Alastair's voice was confident and friendly.

The Billy turned around and gave him a hard stare. His badge read 098. Whether the Billys had been created in an ordered sequence, or if they had all been made at the same time, it didn't matter now.

He would be a new notch. And a new victory in general.

"Officer, I was wondering if you could help me out. See, I'm lost. And I'm gonna be late for work." Alastair got even closer to the cop as he spoke.

"You don't look like you're headed for work. You even have a job?"

Alastair crept in even closer. Close enough to have to look up at the Billy to stare into his eyes. "You misunderstand. I mean, I gotta work, same as everyone. Doesn't matter if we all define it differently."

098 looked at him inquisitively, unsure where this was headed. "What's your point?"

The camera zoomed in further to Alastair's hand reaching up to touch the Billy's chest next to the badge. The Billy's hand shot out and grabbed Alastair's wrist, arresting it in place before he could make contact.

"You'd better keep your hands to yourself, buddy. It's too early for this shit. Don't fuck with me."

"Perhaps you're not getting me. Maybe you've got a job for me."

Now the Billy looked at him with recognition in his eyes and Jacky was sure to catch it all on camera. 098 reached for his belt and unlatched the cuffs.

Alastair didn't resist. "If that's how you want it, that's fine with me." His wrists were still sore, but it didn't matter. "Where do you want me?"

The cop didn't say anything in response but slapped on the cuffs and opened the back door of the patrol car. *Shit! Is he actually gonna take me in? I haven't even had my chance yet.* The Billy pointed to the back seat, not needing any words to convey his meaning.

Across the street Diego started sweating. This was already getting botched up and he thought to intervene. But Alastair had told him to stay put. Jacky let the camera keep rolling, unsure what was going to happen next.

Alastair got in the back seat. The cop entered the front and pulled out his radio. *This isn't good. Oh shit!*

The dispatcher responded over the crackling radio, "Dispatch. Whatcha got 098?"

"Just a heads up, I'm going to be a little late. Car trouble. I should be able to sort it out quickly. Just wanted to let you know I'm on my way as soon as possible. Have 074 cover me, if necessary. Out."

Bingo!

The Billy exited the car once more and, opening the back door, got in. He slid himself over to Alastair, who sat there silently, giving him the eyes. Neither of them said anything. 098 grabbed at Alastair's belt and unbuckling it, yanked if off with one pull. Alastair lifted his ass as he did this, helping him along.

"I'm the one who has to get to work. Let's make this quick." Before he was finished getting the words out, he had Alastair's pants around his knees and his cock in his hand. He stroked it until it started to get hard, and once fully erect, he scootched over making room on the bucket seat between them.

098 leaned down and took Alastair in his mouth. The roughness of his stubble slightly chafing Alastair's skin. He started slow but then sped up and started going deeper. Alastair's head tilted back, wanting to watch but giving in to the feeling, the first time he had been in a Billy's mouth. His thirty-second, but still new and fresh.

The cop's head moved up and down, going faster as he went. Alastair opened his eyes and looked out the window, seeing Jacky move in closer with the camera. Alastair wished his hands were free, so that he could push a little. But the cop was obviously well versed, and Alastair could feel himself getting close. He tilted his head at Jacky, suggesting that he try to move in even closer for the money shot.

Again, his head tilted back as the Billy brought him closer and closer. He couldn't hold it any longer and forgot all about the camera and the set-up, giving in to the intense rapture of orgasm. He busted into 098's mouth who held his position and crammed it in deeper still, prolonging the orgasm until Alastair thought he would shrivel with pleasure.

11

The generic but exciting beat and melody, accompanied by the channel number in big red bold letters, followed a cutaway shot of the city from above, and then immediately cut back to commercial. Alastair tuned out the ads and took a pull from his beer. It had been a long few days and he was bushed. He kicked his feet up on the coffee table, knocking off a few old dead magazines and a full ash-tray. But he was too tired to care. He forced himself to stay up. The beer wasn't helping, but it wasn't hurting either.

In the ad, shiny new cars raced through a clean and empty city. *How the hell do they film these things?* The part of the city was familiar, but he had sure never seen it look like that. The reality was more like tent city and a breeding ground for rats. As if a landfill had been accidently tipped over into the once vibrant downtown and no one had bothered to clean up. Like everyone had forgotten what it could have been like, and nobody cared. He didn't give a damn either, but he did wonder where they hid all of those homeless people and the trash, because wherever they had hidden them, they had leaked right back to their places as soon as the cameras were gone.

The news came back on with some boring story about drought affecting vineyards in the north, with some feel-good ending about tequila growers moving in. Alastair didn't like wine or tequila and spaced out through the rest of the story.

Alastair cracked a fourth beer and nearly spilled it as the next story came on.

"Corruption and scandal in the fourth precinct. Police caught on tape in multiple illegal activities. The new Cops of the Future program at risk after animosity and violence exposed."

The screen flashed to Jacky's footage of the brawl between the normies and the Billys. They had cropped some of the footage to make it look more exciting. And the juiciest bits were repeated as the commentary went on.

"Many officers on the force have signed petitions asking to cancel the program of what many have referred to as 'super-cops' which have been on the streets since March. Early in the program the force welcomed an increase in manpower, but tensions have steadily been rising since, culminating in a riot outside of a local bar."

Again, the images looped, showing the clearest parts of the footage, particularly the parts where you could see officers in uniform throwing blows and the distinct pretty face of the one of the Billys taking a blow.

The way they had framed Jacky's footage and reedited it clearly spoke to the network's angle that the Cops of the Future program should be cancelled. But for now, they were probably soaring with the ratings such a scandal would bring.

"We go now to Police Chief Oberton for an inside peek at what the force is doing about the recent unrest."

The camera cut to the Chief on the steps of the

downtown station, the same where the boys had scored weed just the other day.

"While we abhor violence of any kind, we're not surprised something like this has happened. We need *real* cops on the streets, not some freak imitation."

The scene cut away from the Police Chief to a regular uniform cop with the news commentator introducing the man as Lieutenant Daniels.

"These new cops from the Cops of the Future program have been a major disturbance to the force. Not only do they not get along with the guys, but they've taken a zealous approach to fighting crime, one which has made the citizens of this city unduly nervous. That's not our idea of how to fight crime effectively."

The picture now went back to the commentator in the studio with the footage of the brawl showing behind them.

"This next clip may offend some viewers. Viewer discretion advised."

The TV now showed shaky camera footage approaching the patrol car in the parking lot behind the bar. There he was, Alastair cuffed in the back of the car with the Billy on top of him. Thick black censored bars covered both of their faces and the rest of the not-fit-for-TV bits.

While he knew this was coming, Alastair couldn't believe that he was on TV. Especially not with what was being shown. He felt himself start to rise seeing the scene from another vantage point. Setting his beer down with one hand, he freed himself from his pants with the other. They weren't going to show much, but they didn't need to; he remembered the moment with 098 well. Cock now in his hand he stroked it quickly, not wanting to miss their moment displayed so publicly. Somehow it was even hotter seeing it vicariously. Whatever the news anchor was saying went in one ear and right out the other as his pace quickened and he shot his load all over the floor in front of his recliner.

In his moment of reliving that fast and deep head, he had totally missed what was being said in response to the scene being caught on tape and flaunted as reasoning for getting rid of the Billys. Whatever it was it looked as if the department were coming apart from within. Apparently, the regular cops were all thrilled about the public shaming, but were also having to save face about the riot. Although now they were looking justified in what they had done due to the footage being shown back-to-back.

The anchor came back on the screen momentarily. "In defense of the Cops of the Future program we now bring you Retired Captain Dale Thompson."

The screen went to a new face. One so handsome Alastair could never forget it, although older than he had ever seen it before. It was a Billy. That same chiseled jaw, that irresistible brow and broad shoulders.

"We initiated the Cops of the Future program as an experiment, one which has met with much undue fear and criticism. And despite this recent tragedy, crime rates in the city have steadily gone down since the introduction of the program. We can't let isolated incidents of misconduct be an indicator of the success of the program."

He was only on the screen for a moment, and then he disappeared into the minutiae of the rest of the newscast. *So we have our Golden Goose. And his name! And while the city is going nuts it's my chance. We've got to find him!*

12

"Yeah, and how are we gonna find him? It's not like they're gonna advertise where the guy lives." Diego was dubious. He looked over to Jacky, who nodded in agreement.

To show his further agreement Jacky chimed in, "Besides, even if we did know where he lived there's no way that we could just walk right up to the front door. That guy is a celebrity after being on the news. Everybody knows who he is now." He set his beer down on the table between the three of them, crammed some peanuts in his mouth and continued talking with his mouth full, "There'll probably be cops everywhere. And Billy Club."

Alastair gazed around the bar, confident that no one was listening in on their conversation. "You guys don't think I've thought of all that? Come on. You know me. The answer was right there in the news as well. Daniels is gonna tell us where he lives. He's got access and he's got a reason. You saw how much that guy hates the Billys. Enough to get in bed with us. And as far as cops swarming the place goes, I'm counting on it. They probably figure the guy needs protection, but not from us. It's the regular fuzz that they'd be worried about." He stood up and pointed to the television, even though it wasn't on. "You saw it all right there. There's a war going on. And we...we get to play on both sides."

Recognition spread across their faces. Alastair was right about the larger issues with the force. The cops would be distracted. Not only did they need to save face publicly, but within the department there was sure to be turmoil. They were facing greater scrutiny, so why would they bother with a few street thugs when they were facing disaster within.

"Bartender, bring us three more," Alastair shouted across the room, "I think it's time to do a little celebrating. Not only did our movies make it all the way to the news, but now nobody is gonna trust these fuckers as far as they can throw them. And for us, I got two words: *Golden Goose*."

❧ 13 ❧

The street was filled with the usual riff raff; the blocks leading up to the station were still the place to score weed. A few blocks in any direction, if you knew which, would lead you into just about anything you wanted. Crime prevention at its best. Every so often they would round everyone up and rotate the dealers, switching what was available on which block. To the causal observer it would look like the streets had cleaned up a bit. But every junky and hustler instinctively knew to move along with the flow. Regular cop and Billy alike looked the other way, and the heat from city officials would die down for a bit. It was a system that appeared to work even though nothing really changed.

Alastair laughed to himself as he saw street boys selling ass on the corner across from the guy moving his hand in a gesture that meant "barbies." The smell of swag weed drifted by; everything was in order, the city running the way it always did. The only real difference today was that he was heading *toward* the station. Not something he would normally sign up for. He was risking his ass walking straight in. Someone might recognize him from the video. Surely they had all seen the uncensored version of the film that had played on the news. But this time, visiting the station, he had one thing on his side. He hadn't actually committed a crime, at least not one that anybody was chasing him for. And there was no way he was gonna send either of the guys up here for this job. Those bumblers would not know how to talk to the cops even if their absent fathers had beat it into them.

For a moment he paused at the steps leading up to the station. The same steps where Daniels had stood the day before denouncing the Billys. The city was ripe to pop, and he was in the middle of it all, standing in the exact spot where the first volley had been fired. The shot had been only words, but it had been fired. With tensions running so high it was impossible not to get hot about it. All the while right on the doorstep of the enemy.

He strode into the station without incident. Regular cops and plain clothes cops filled the bustling hallway leading up to the reception desk. A few Billys were peppered among the crowd, but he couldn't get close enough to see if he recognized any badge numbers. Besides, that would have to wait; they weren't part of this mission, yet.

In front of him two beat cops were roughly leading their catch to the booking desk. How many times had Alastair found himself in that poor schmuck's position? But this time he wasn't heading to the booking desk. He walked freely up to the receptionist and announced his visit, several minutes before his appointment was due to start.

Putting down the phone and looking at the appointment book, the man at the desk directed Alastair to the stairs that led up to the offices. It was a part of the station he had never seen, and it was the first time he had walked freely through the station, at least on his way in rather than out.

He found Daniels' office door slightly ajar and

knocked without crossing the threshold. Everything was riding on this meeting, and it had to go well. Being forceful wasn't going to work. He had to let Daniels be in charge. Typical cop mentality, one that was so predictable that it was easy to play.

"Enter." His voice was gruffer than it had been on TV, a sign that at times he could try to appear likeable. No veneer here. "Close the door behind you."

Alastair slowly entered and walked up to the desk extending his hand for a shake. Daniels looked at him with contempt and gestured for him to sit, without returning the friendly gesture.

Taking control of the situation Daniels started the conversation like an interrogation, "I don't like you being here and I don't want you to feel welcome. Let's get that straight right from the beginning." Alastair nodded. "We have one thing in common and one thing only. So, get right to the point."

Alastair could appreciate the no nonsense, right to business attitude. He imagined that Daniels was a top, that he would take control of any situation, more comfortable in the driver's seat than anywhere else.

"I won't take up too much of your time, officer. I think you know who I am just as well as I know who you are. So, yeah, I'll get right to the point. It seems that we have a common interest." He looked around the office trying to identify if there might be any indication of further commonality, but saw none. "All I want is Thompson's address."

Daniels had a smug look on his face, aware that he held all of the power in the situation. "Yeah, and what would you do with that? Wait, I don't want to know. You're part of the so-called Billy Club, right?"

Alastair nodded.

"Thought so. I recognize you from the video, probably from the street too. And what are you going to do for me if I help you out?"

A thousand images flashed through Alastair's mind. Something about being in the station on his own free will got him all flushed.

"I think we both want the same thing," Alastair said, "and, no offense, but I'm in the position to be a bit more discreet than you are. No position to risk, as it were."

Daniels nodded in agreement, but didn't want to hand anything over without a fight. He would never relinquish control to street trash like Alastair. Never. But he couldn't have organized for a better arrangement than this to discredit the Billys so soon after the shit had hit the fan.

Alastair looked around the office again, zeroing in on the family portrait that sat on Daniels' desk, complete with wife, kids, and the family dog. This was the kind of man who thought he was so in control of himself that he wasn't gay as long as he didn't have anything put into him. The *just because I moved a lawn once, doesn't make me a gardener* type.

Under Daniels' hard stare Alastair got down on the ground and crawled under the desk. He knew Daniels would get into it, as long as he could pretend he was somewhere else, with someone else. Alastair didn't care. This would only sweeten his victory. He had no feelings for the man. Just another target in the war.

He let Daniels take down his own uniform blues, letting the man maintain his sense of control. He kept his hands to his side, using only his mouth, completing the illusion of total authority. At first Daniels' body was rigid, almost as stiff as his cock. But as Alastair moved with his mouth the cop began to slack in his chair, slouching ever so slightly, but trying to stay upright should anyone walk by and see.

Alastair started to move quicker but Daniels took his head in his hands and forced him to move at his desired pace. One hand on each side of his head he moved it up and down the way he wanted it. Hard thrusts, one by one, in a jerking motion. Apparently, he didn't like the smooth up and down, but rather the slow jackhammer.

He took his time. One forceful push after the other until he erupted, cramming his cock all the way in so that the cum missed Alastair's tongue altogether and slid down his throat, no choice but to swallow.

"You got what you came for. It's right there on that paper on the desk. Now get the fuck out of my office. Now."

Alastair did as he was told, but left the office with a strut he hadn't had on the way in.

The place wasn't surrounded like they had thought it would be but there were several patrol cars parked in the driveway and one out back. The cops, all Billys, were milling about the property, but they looked unsure what to do or why they were stationed there. Apparently, the force didn't think the situation was terribly important. Two of them stood near the doorway drinking coffee, the tone of their conversation didn't sound like they anticipated any issues.

It was always a bit strange to see two or more of them. They were like identical twins, but not just in their looks; their mannerisms, the way they held themselves, everything was identical. Except for the badge numbers. They couldn't get a close up look to tell, but today it didn't matter. They were here to see the Golden Goose.

Jacky had his camera and looked a little nervous. Diego was jacked up on something and was reeling to go, moving from foot to foot as he always did when he was worked up.

"You guys need to chill the fuck out if we're going to get past those Billys and inside." Alastair spoke slowly and calmly, hoping to have the same effect on the guys. "We're going to have to wait until there's only one of them in front. There's no way we'll get past both of them."

The three of them waited behind a hedge, just out of sight from the direction the cops were looking. The neighborhood was quiet, and not a regular cop was in sight. Other than the patrol cars there was a sparkling new Porsche in the driveway. Dale Thompson must have done well for himself selling off his likeness. With any luck they'd be able to snag a few things on their way out and sweeten the deal.

"Look at this place. This guy must be loaded. Didn't think being a cop paid this well." Diego said.

Jacky chimed in, half whispering, "The TV said he was retired. Maybe he got into another line of work."

"Don't be a fool. It's obviously this Cops of the Future thing that made him flush. Don't forget why we're here. We need to get footage of a hookup. Bring the whole motherfucker crashing down on them. Take some shit on the way out if you can. But only if we have time." Alastair stuck his fingers into their chests as he spoke.

He must have raised his voice because the Billys quieted down for a moment and started looking around. All three of them hit the ground and scuttled under the hedge before they could be seen. One of the Billys said something into his radio and went back to drinking coffee and chatting with his fellow officer. There was no sign of Thompson, but he had to be there. They had seen nobody come or go and they'd been casing the place for hours.

Alastair put his finger to his mouth, silently shushing the guys. They were too close to blow it now. The Billy from out back came around to the front, swinging his flashlight beam left to right across the yard, at waist level, fortunately, sweeping right over them laying there on the ground. He moved over to the other Billys and said something. They were too far away to make out the words but could see the other cop shaking his head no. Whatever they were taking about was resolved soon for the conversation didn't last long. The third Billy returned to his post behind the mansion.

The Billys out front looked bored. A perfect contrast to the restlessness of the three boys in the bushes. Diego could hardly stop himself from squirming and Alastair gave him a boot to settle him down. One of the cops in front tipped his hat to the other and got back into his patrol car, settling into the driver's seat and fiddling with his radio. But he didn't start the car. The remaining guy in front settled in by the front door, coffee in hand, nonchalantly taking in the scene in front of the house.

In a whisper Alastair said, "I think we're gonna have to try and get in through the back. We're not going to be able to distract the guy on guard at the door and the one in the car at the same time."

The others nodded in agreement. They hadn't been sure of the best way in, but neither had they expected there to be more than an officer or two to guard the place. Jacky was looking more nervous than ever, but Diego was still reeling to go. Whatever he had taken sure filled him with energy.

"Diego. Do you think you can handle him? He's alone back there. I think it's our only chance. We can go in through the back if you can coax him away. Even just for a few minutes. We'll worry about getting out once we've done what we came to do." Even in hushed tones Alastair sounded urgent. All three of them were anxious to get this over with.

Diego stirred. "Yeah, Sure. Just watch my back in case anything happens. If he doesn't go for it you're gonna have to distract him, so I can get away." He was starting to get up but was cautiously waiting for the go ahead.

"Do it. Me and Jacky got your back. Act like your life depends on it. Get a notch while you're at it. Bored Billys are easy prey. Get him."

Alastair gave him a little shove with his boot signaling for him to go while the Billy at the front door was looking the other way. They couldn't see the face of the Billy in the car but had to count on him being distracted. It was now or never.

Diego scuttled out of the bushes and army-crawled toward the back. Still in the bushes Jacky and Alastair held their breath as they watched Diego make his way around the house, skipping into the neighbor's yard, so that he could look to the Billy as if he had approached through the alley.

Good thinking, Diego, for once. Get him.

Once Diego got to the street they lost sight of him. They would just have to pray that the timing worked out. Alastair looked at his watch. "Let's give him ten minutes. If he can't make it happen in that time, we'll have to figure something else out."

The uncertainty made Jacky's jitters even worse. It was visible all over him, even in the dark.

"Get it together. You know what we have to do. All according to plan. We got this."

They sat in silence, the only sound, their breathing. Both were counting in their heads.

Once in the alley Diego stood up and looked around. Fortunately, the street was deserted. To the north the alley led up to the back driveway where the third cop car was parked. The Billy leaned up against the hood, coffee in his hand, gazing off into space. It wasn't going to get any better than this.

Diego puffed out his chest and tried to stoke his bravado. One foot in front of the other he stepped into the driveway.

"Hey. You there. What do you think you're doing?"

The Billy caught sight of him as soon as he hit the pavement of the driveway.

"Oh. Hi, officer. I was wondering if you could give me hand. I was out for a walk, and I seem to have gotten lost. I was on my way..." Before Diego could finish the Billy was right on top of him.

"This is private property. Get lost."

Diego took one step back and thought about running, but this was the moment. "I didn't mean to trespass. Like I said, I got lost out walking." He knew that he didn't fit in with the neighborhood and it was probably obvious to the cop. But then he saw the badge number glisten in the streetlight. #023. One he'd never had. It ignited him with new courage. "I was wondering if maybe you could give me a ride back to the main boulevard? I'm sure I could make it worth your while."

The Billy gave him that hard cop stare, but it was filled with recognition beneath the threatening intensity.

"I can't give you a ride anywhere. I'm on duty."

"Well, maybe I can still make it worth your while." Diego was happy for the speed coursing through his veins. He might not otherwise have had the courage to keep it up.

For a moment the cop was confused, then he regained his composure and reached for his night stick.

Diego took another step back, then pivoted and moved forward a step. "No need for that. Just little old me minding my own business. It must be kind of boring, standing around here all night by yourself." He cautiously moved another step forward and slowly put his hand on the Billy's chest.

The cop didn't move but his eyes were sizing Diego up and down. For a moment it felt like everything was going to come crashing down and then he said, "Ok. But not here. Let's move down the alley a bit."

He had taken the bait.

Diego led the way as they moved down the alley a few blocks, finding a retaining wall they could duck behind. Unsure how long the guys would need, he got down on his hands and knees and slid his pants down just enough to invite the Billy, not wanting to waste any time.

The Billy took the cue and unzipped his fly, rubbing his cock till it hardened enough to get it in Diego's ass. He mounted him and thrust it in dry, eliciting a deep grunt from Diego. He wasn't gentle and pounded as hard as he could, each ramming thrust heading further into Diego's insides. He worked like a machine, an unrelenting piston designed for one thing alone. Diego did his best not to cry out too loud. The last thing they needed was to draw the attention of the men out front. Biting his lip, he let the Billy work on him in steady rhythm.

Alastair looked at his watch again. "I think it's time. Let's go!"

They slipped out of the bushes and quickly made their way to the back door. Unsurprisingly it was locked. Wasting no time, Alastair pulled a rag from out of his pocket and picked up a garden rock. He put the rag up to the back window and brought the rock crashing through it as quietly as he could. It shattered inwards and he reached through to unlock the handle.

"Now. Start filming. He's probably upstairs."

Neither of them could believe that they were this close to the Golden Goose. And neither knew what to expect.

Jacky turned on the video camera, and they moved through the dark downstairs of the house, looking for a way up. They moved down a hallway filled with family pictures. In the faint light coming from the windows, they could see some of the photos.

"Alastair, look. This guy has a family. Looks like a wife and kids."

"Bullshit. It has to be a beard."

"Seriously though, maybe this isn't a good idea."

"Trust me. We've come too far to back out now."

At the end of the hallway, they found the stairs. At the top they could see a door with a sliver of light projecting from the crack at the bottom.

"Follow my lead. I'll move in first. All you have to do is get it on tape."

Slowly they crept up the stairs toward the door. As Alastair reached for the handle it slammed open. Dale burst through the door, .45 in hand. He swung the gun through the darkness searching for the intruder. Alastair hit the floor and rolled back down the stairs knocking Jacky off his feet. The sound registered on Dale's face, and he fired toward the direction of the noise. Two, then three shots rang out and Alastair's ears rang like he'd been hit in the head. He rolled the rest of the way back down the stairs and booked it back toward the door they had come in.

Once he was back out in the driveway he took off down the alley to the south until he found a dumpster with an open lid. He leapt inside and closed the lid as quietly as possible. He waited as silently as he could, straining to hear any sign of Jacky. The alley was as cold as the grave. He'd been within inches of the Golden Goose, and everything had gone wrong.

After a while sirens cut through the air. He could feel the rumble of patrol cars passing the dumpster, but none stopped to investigate. He waited until sunrise. Agonizing hours passed and still no sign of Jacky, or Diego for that matter. Jacky had probably taken a bullet. Who knew about Diego...

It had been a disaster. But if the Golden Goose had killed Jacky, the Cops of the Future program was definitely up.

🎇 15 🎇

It was all over the news. The headlines were lurid, and public anger was at an all-time high. Daniels and many other regular cops frequently appeared publicly denouncing the Billys and how their program model was an unhinged safety risk. Police violence was on everyone's lips. No one cared about the numbers about crime rates being down, not with the cops killing civilians.

Alastair watched it all unfold on the TV in the bar. The force was unraveling. Hatred toward the Billys was palpable. The vitriol wasn't just coming from the old school guys on the force; the public was demanding an end to the Cops of the Future program in the city. And he was nowhere near to the hundred notches he had set out for.

Fucking cops. Always ruining everything. Even when they *are the good thing.*

They never said his name, but the news confirmed that the intruder at the Golden Goose's house had been killed in an act of self-defense. The fact that the house had been under surveillance and protection was only used as one more excuse why the Billys were ineffectual. And the news played the clips of the brawl and the scene in the car over and over again, to drive the point home. Hot as it was watching the cop suck his cock over and over again, they censored all the juicy bits. The fact that his face was somewhat recognizable in the footage did have its perks, it brought with it fanboys who all wanted a piece of the most famous member of the Billy Club.

As fun as it was, they were no Billys. And while the program was axed in the city, it didn't mean that it wasn't still going strong in other areas.

Maybe it's time for a move to another city. New streets, new cops. Same M.O..

ABOUT THE AUTHORS

J. W. Steed is a pseudonym for the author of more than a dozen mainstream novels. He also writes memoir and humorous essays. He teaches creative writing in the metro NYC area and is active in the Science Fiction and Fantasy Writer's Association (SFWA). Steed made his paperback debut in the bestseller <u>Dirty Dorms and Fresh Men</u>. He has a cult following who can't wait to read more! You can read Mr. Steed's blog at mrsteed64.blogspot.com

Frank Slater pops in from time to time. He is a historian of mid-twenty-first century science fiction and has been involved in the creation of the retrospective oral history of speculative arts project, *Hindsight*. When not moving through the temporal sphere, he has occasionally partaken in writing science fiction. Much of his work is forthcoming, but his stories have also appeared in *Simultaneous Times* and various critical journals.

OTHER BOOKS FROM PETER SCHUTES PUBLISHING

Please visit Peter's Website to find links to all of Peter's books.

E-books and Paperbacks

The Able Seaman

The Anaconda Copper

The Autobiography of Peter Schutes

Backwoods Delivery

Big Bodies of All Sizes

Big Hole River

Bobbing Buoys and Salty Seamen

Buck Private

Bunkhouse Buddies

The Butt Baby

Chopper Jock

Cloistered

Coached

Confessions of a Rodeo Clown

Cosmic Cage

Dark as a Dungeon

Demonic Deception *aka* Deceived, Cursed & Blessed

Desert Island Daddies

Dirty Cop

Dirty Dorms and Fresh Men

Dormitory Urges

Dutch Treat

Enjambment

The Expectant Member

Filthy Jobs and Steamy Showers

Firehouse Lovers

The Fish

Five Erotic Tales

The Gospel of Priapus

Hardhats and Nightsticks

Hercules and Lippos

Hobo Honey

Hoboes, Hustlers, and Outlaws

Hot Blue Collars

Hotshot

In Each Other's Arms

Kwiklube 5000

Like the Greeks Do

Little Shamus

Logger's Delight

Muscle Beach

Muscle Bottom

One Eternal Day

The Orchardman

Panama Heat

Satanic Seductions

Satan's Sissy Boy

The Slaves of Rome

Sleazy A

Small Cockpits and Big Hangars

The Spotter

Steroid Steve

Tales of Two Daddies

The Tearoom in the Trees

The Thigh Baby

Under the Boardwalk

Wee Dobbin

World's Biggest

***** Coming Soon *****

More Tales of Two Daddies

Mowing and Blowing

Come Young and Come Old